CROSSING THE PANTHER'S PATH

Also by Elizabeth Alder

THE KING'S SHADOW

Elizabeth Alder

CROSSING THE
PANTHER'S PATH

FARRAR STRAUS GIROUX • NEW YORK

Copyright © 2002 by Elizabeth Alder
Map copyright © 2002 by Susan Weizer-Clair
All rights reserved
Distributed in Canada by Douglas & McIntyre Ltd.
Printed in the United States of America
Designed by Robbin Gourley
First edition, 2002
1 3 5 7 9 10 8 6 4 2

Library of Congress Cataloging-in-Publication Data
Alder, Elizabeth.
   Crossing the panther's path / Elizabeth Alder.— 1st ed.
   p. cm.
   Summary: Sixteen-year-old Billy Calder, son of a British soldier and a Mohawk
woman, leaves school to join Tecumseh in his efforts to prevent the Americans
from taking any more land from the Indians in the Northwest Territory.
   ISBN 0-374-31662-7
   1. Caldwell, Billy, 1780–1841—Juvenile fiction.   2. Tecumseh, Shawnee Chief,
1768–1813—Juvenile fiction.   [1. Caldwell, Billy, 1780–1841—Fiction.
2. Tecumseh, Shawnee Chief, 1768–1813—Fiction.   3. Indians of North
America—Fiction.   4. United States—History—War of 1812—Fiction.]   I. Title.

PZ7.A3612 Cr 2002
[Fic]—dc21

                                                                    2001054483

Dedicated to my father and mother,
Robert and Angela Clair

CONTENTS

Author's Note *ix*

1 The Town of Detroit on the Northwest Frontier 5
2 A Straight Tree Rooted in Two Worlds 16
3 The Medicine Bag Has Lost Its Power 23
4 The Panther's Men and the King's Men
Will Fight Again 38
5 *Ad Majorem Dei Gloriam* 46
6 The Gorging Wolf Eats Our Land 51
7 A Bundle of Sticks Is Strong 70
8 I Have Spoken 84
9 The Very Ground Will Tremble 94
10 Tippecanoe 111
11 A Spy among the Long Knives 118
12 A Deadly Game of Riddles 135
13 The Battle for Detroit 150
14 A World Rimmed with Frost and Snow 164
15 Saints and Snow Snakes 176
16 Go and Put On Petticoats 185
17 Before All the Leaves Fall 198
18 *Weshecat-too-weh* 207
19 The White Road of Peace 219

Epilogue 228

AUTHOR'S NOTE

Two hundred years ago, the vast land in the northern United States between the Ohio and Mississippi Rivers was coveted by many nations. The American Indians regarded it as their sacred homeland, the British and the French wanted it for the valuable fur trade, and the Americans saw it as potential farmland. Tecumseh, an Ohio-born Shawnee war chief, vowed to regain the land that was taken from his people following the Battle of Fallen Timbers in 1794. His goal was to halt the westward expansion of the United States. In this attempt he succeeded in forging a vast confederation of tribes. A brilliant military genius who embodied courage and compassion, Tecumseh inspired intense loyalty among his followers. He drew to himself a fascinating circle of advisers, allies, and aides. Among them was a young linguist named Billy Caldwell. It is Billy's life that inspired this book.

In *Crossing the Panther's Path*, I have tried to remain as close as possible to historical fact. I'm grateful to librarians both here in the United States and in Canada for their generous assistance while I was researching this time period. The following were notably helpful: Mary Farrell, former Director of Tribal Rolls and Archives for the Citizen Band Potawatomi Indians of Oklahoma; Emily Clark of the Chicago Historical Society; the Western Reserve Historical Society Library; and the Ministry of Citizenship, Culture and Recreation, Archives of Ontario. Any errors that remain are purely my own. In addition, thanks go to Marianne Slattery and Robert and Angela Clair for reading the manuscript and offering suggestions. Finally, I am most grateful to my agent, Alison Picard, for her perseverance and my editor, Robbie Mayes, for his kind and thoughtful assistance.

CROSSING THE PANTHER'S PATH

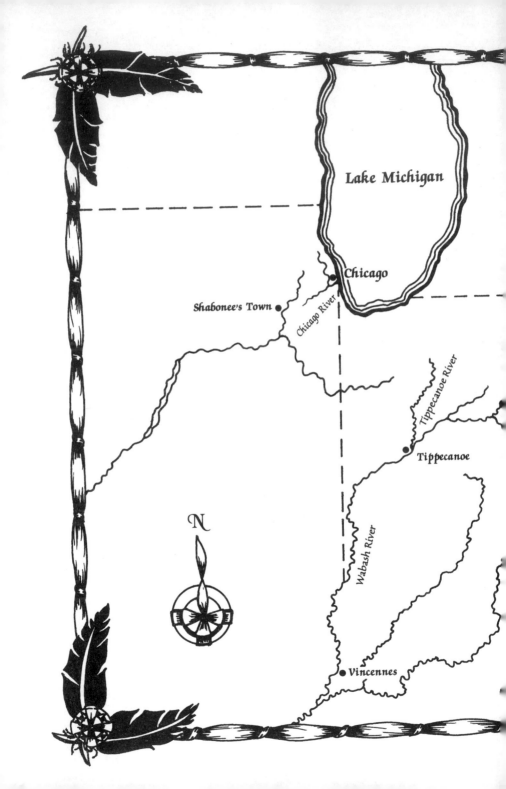

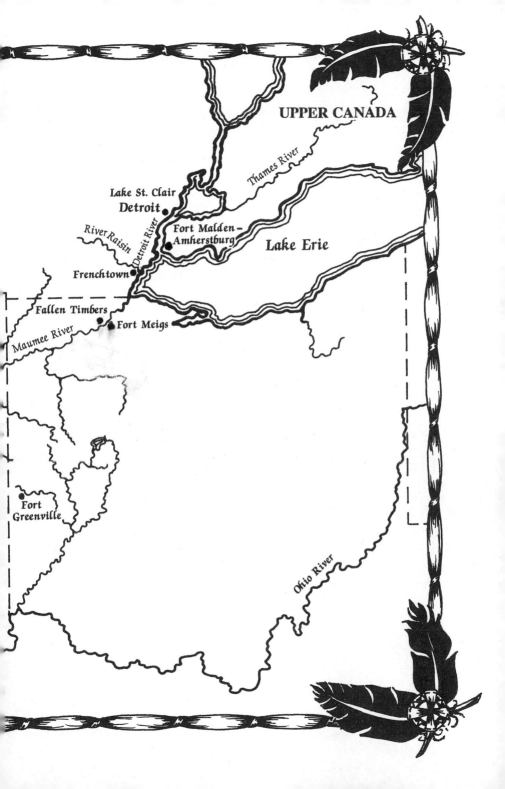

1 · THE TOWN OF DETROIT ON THE NORTHWEST FRONTIER

December 1809

*B*illy Calder peered into the brutish and dirt-streaked faces of the fur trappers and wondered if he could possibly trust them. The two men were already mounted on their shaggy horses and seemed impatient to be on their way. One led a packhorse loaded with many bundles. Despite his suspicions, Billy swung up into his saddle determined to make the perilous journey.

"Snow will come with this wind before nightfall," Père Jean-Paul warned Billy. The French-born Jesuit spoke in heavily accented English as he held the bridle of Billy's mare to steady her. With his leathery face lifted to the sky, his hooked nose resembled the beak of an eagle.

Billy cast a glance at the dark clouds galloping overhead. The raw air smelled of snow. He swallowed hard, knowing full well the danger into which he rode. The first blizzard of the season looked to be a severe one, and there would be no inns, no shelter of any kind, between here and his destination.

"It's only a ride of three hours," he countered, in an effort to reassure his teacher. "We'll be there before nightfall."

Père Jean-Paul shook his head doubtfully. He'd been in the wilderness many years; the harsh winters had turned his face into a spiderweb of lines. "You are bullheaded, as the Redcoats say. It is easy to become lost in such a storm."

"I have to go," Billy said. "My father's letter said to come."

"You're excited to see your mother, *non?*" the missionary asked.

Billy nodded. "It's been two years," he said. "She is visiting my father now at Amherstburg. If I don't leave soon, I may be snowed in here at Detroit."

"You are certain, *n'est-ce pas?*" Père Jean-Paul said with a sigh. "Very well, then, go, *et Dieu vous garde.*"

"God be with you also," Billy said.

The missionary hesitated before handing the bridle to Billy. Reaching into one of his deep pockets, he brought out a small loaf of bread wrapped in cloth. "Should you need it . . ." he said. Billy thanked him and tucked it in his satchel.

"We have to go," one trapper said curtly through tobacco-stained teeth. Like the black robe, he and his partner were French-born. Called voyageurs, they roamed the untamed wilderness farther west in search of pelts. They'd come east to sell their goods. A quarrelsome pair, they'd agreed to take the boy with them only because a countryman had asked.

"*Oui, bien sûr,*" Père Jean-Paul said, stepping back. "Keep safe."

The three riders made their way through the narrow streets of Detroit past a cooper's stall, a blacksmith's shop, and John Kinzie's trading post. The windswept lanes were deserted except for a few townspeople hurrying from shop to shop. As the riders entered the main street, a family of Indians moved out of the path of the horses. Like others before them, they had come to the white man's town desperately seeking food. Billy knew they were of the Miami tribe by the quillwork on their moccasins. They must have walked all the way from northwestern Ohio, he thought. He gazed into the thin face of a little boy bundled on his mother's back. The child stared back through large frightened eyes. He looked as if it had been several days since he'd eaten. Billy gave the woman his loaf of bread. They needed it more than he did. She thanked him, and he replied in her own language. Then he caught up with the trappers, who'd ridden ahead, and together they made their way downhill to the river.

One trapper, a bearded fellow who was leading the heavily burdened packhorse, cursed under his breath. Wrapped in a coat banded in white and red, he cleared his throat and spit. The other wore Indian buckskins, fringed and ornamented with quillwork. On his head was a long woolen cap that flopped over. A bright red tassel swung from its tip.

"You should have gotten two packhorses," he said sharply.

"If I'd gotten another packhorse, you'd complain that I spent too much money," the bearded man said.

The buckskin-clad trapper grumbled about the poor prices the Americans had offered them in Detroit.

"The British merchants of Amherstburg will deal with us fairly," he said.

"They are swindlers, too," his companion muttered sourly.

Billy saw that there would be no friendship offered here, and he kept quiet. The Frenchmen made it clear that they hated the

British and resented the upstart Americans who now ruled much of the lake country.

As they left the town, the travelers were engulfed in a magnificent scene of wintry desolation. Brown earth and pewter sky stretched before them in muted shades. The leaves had long since been blown from the trees, and the bare branches raked the sky sullenly. Wind-driven snow began to rush across the wild landscape. They rode in silence now, slightly on edge, for they knew the danger into which they journeyed. Soon the river came into view with its cold gunmetal-gray water swiftly flowing past.

They dismounted at the shore and tugged their skittish horses aboard a flat-bottomed ferryboat. A scowling waterman, roused from the shelter of his little wooden shack, poled them across the wide Detroit River. When the water became too deep for the pole, he worked the rudder, fighting the current that struggled to pull them downriver into Lake Erie. Before setting them on the shore of British-held Upper Canada, the waterman warned them grimly, "Mind you, now. This storm bodes ill."

They rode due south toward the town of Amherstburg and nearby Fort Malden. The wind nipped Billy's ears, and he pulled his wool cap down. Although he was fond of his black robe teachers and grateful to have a chance to attend the Jesuit boarding school in Detroit, he was glad to be away. He wanted only to hurry his mare toward the town where his father and mother were awaiting his arrival. He was disappointed now to find these voyageurs in such a quarrelsome mood, and with the blizzard fast approaching, it promised to be a longer journey than he had anticipated.

"You should have tied the furs better," the man in the buckskins and tasseled cap yelled over the wind.

"They are tied well enough," the bearded trapper answered defensively.

"We cannot afford to lose any." The man in the buckskins spoke with growing irritation. "I assure you, we will not be allowed to trade with our old friends the Miami now that the Americans are settling Ohio."

"Ils sont si stupides qu'on ne peut rien faire d'eux," the bearded man argued.

His partner snorted in disgust. "You think they are so stupid that nothing can be done with them? You think they cannot keep us out? Why do you think the Americans have built so many forts? *Un, deux, trois, quatre, cinq . . ."* he began counting.

And as he did so, Billy began naming them silently: Fort Harmar, Fort Washington, Fort St. Clair, Fort Jefferson, Fort Greenville, Fort Defiance.

"There are at least six between the Ohio Rivière and Erie du Lac," the Frenchman continued. "Are they there to invite us in? I don't think so. The Americans are not so stupid. Look how they took Detroit from the British just as the British took it from France."

"You worry too much. This does not concern us," the man with the beard said.

"Ah, there you are wrong," the man in the buckskins said, jabbing his finger in the air as if to make his point more strongly. "We will not be trapping for long if the American settlers continue to drive their wagons over the Appalachian Mountains."

Billy listened intently. This concerned him, too. His father, an Irish officer in the British King's army, had once been stationed in Fort Detroit, the fortress now ruled by the Americans. Billy had to cross the river into Canada if he wished to see him.

"We are beaten," the man in the buckskins said. "The lake country is slipping away from us. There are few of us. We take some beaver pelts or elk hides to trade, and then we leave. But the Americans are many. They are farmers. They come to settle. You wait and see."

The boy shrank into his coat, hoping to stay warm. He could understand why these Frenchmen were filled with hate. It was their countrymen who first mapped the rivers and streams and traded cloth and guns for beaver pelts from the Indians. Later, when the British learned there was money to be had in the fur trade, they claimed the lake country for themselves. The old fort built by the French on the Detroit River, which connected Lake St. Clair and Lake Erie, was taken by the powerful Redcoats.

Now it was the Americans who were staking their claim. Hungry for land, the colonists had ignored King George's proclamation in 1763 forbidding settlement west of the Appalachians. They crossed the mountains and steered their rafts down the Ohio River. They built their cabins in the hunting grounds of Kentucky. After winning their independence from Britain, the colonists grew even bolder, landing their boats north of the river. When the Shawnee and Miami protested, the Americans answered by building forts along the Ohio River and deep into Indian territory.

When the packhorse slipped on a patch of ice, the bearded trapper cursed the poor animal and jerked its lead rope cruelly.

Billy listened as the Frenchman discussed their situation in low tones in his own language. His partner cast a quick side-long glance at Billy before nodding almost imperceptibly, in agreement with some devious plan.

So they want to steal my horse to use as a second pack animal, do they? Billy thought. *Just let them try.*

Soon the packhorse was steady on its feet again, and Billy urged his own beloved Kumari onward. The mare was a strong bay with a white blaze on her forehead like a diadem. She had been a gift from his father and he had explained that her name meant "princess" in a land to the east where British sea captains bought tea. *No one's taking Kumari from me.* From then on, it seemed to Billy that the trappers watched him through cold, narrowed eyes, waiting for an opportunity, and he was careful to keep some distance from them.

Snow continued to fall, and before they'd traveled far, the wet flakes filled the wagon ruts in the frozen road. Stinging wind made his eyes water as Billy squinted into the distance. The cold cut through his coat, and his lungs ached from the frigid air. Landmarks disappeared in the swirling snow, and although he had made this journey before, the country now seemed alien to him. They must reach Amherstburg before darkness fell. If they had simply followed the river, they would have found it easily, but an hour after they left Detroit the road curved eastward away from the bottom land.

The trappers shouted at each other in French studded with words from strange Indian tongues they'd learned west of the great river. Billy tried to shut their talk from his ears. More than ever he longed to be home, where his father, a man accustomed to giving orders and being obeyed, had no need to raise his voice.

Towering maple and oak trees crowded the woods through

which they rode. Evergreen hemlocks guarded the ravines where stony brooks had frozen over. Twice they spotted deer prints in the fresh snow, and once, in the distance, Billy caught the swift blur of a red fox fleeing at their approach.

As they moved from the forest to an open meadow, the trail disappeared, and there was neither sun nor moon by which to steer a course. Snow spun around them in whirlwinds, and Billy halted in an effort to get his bearings. Patting the thick fur of Kumari's neck, he peered into the whiteness. He saw nothing familiar. The mare seemed puzzled that they had stopped. She stamped her hooves impatiently. One of the trappers nodded in the direction he thought was south.

"Non, mon ami," the other answered in French, pointing in another direction.

The wind soughed menacingly.

They began to bicker again.

"It's this way," Billy interrupted them.

His traveling companions looked at him in surprise, as if startled by the boy's voice. But he had spoken with such assurance that they seemed inclined to trust him, at least for a time. The three riders entered another stand of trees as darkness closed in around them. After a while, however, the bearded trapper grumbled in French that they had been fools to have listened to a boy. They would all surely freeze to death in this blizzard. Billy himself began to wonder if he had misled them.

Black tree trunks loomed through the deepening twilight as they urged their horses onward. The wind roared, and creaking branches swayed perilously overhead. In the distance, they heard the sharp *crack* of a tree limb as it snapped.

More time passed, and Billy caught himself dozing, half-frozen in his saddle. He knew he must stay awake—if he fell asleep, they would shove him from his saddle and disappear with Kumari. The leather reins felt stiff as metal in his palms, and his feet had grown ice-cold in the stirrups. He wriggled his toes inside his black boots. He rubbed his hands to restore some feeling to his numb fingertips and pulled his sleeves down over his knuckles.

The bearded trapper spit in the snow and cried out, "Why did we leave Detroit? These furs will do us no good if we die. Let's stop. We can build a fire." He roughly reined his horse to a halt.

"The town is near," Billy said. "I know it."

He could see by their faces that they had no confidence in him. The man in the white-and-red coat was convinced they would all die. He wanted to stop and build a lean-to shelter. His complaining voice filled Billy's ears. Billy was worried, too. Each year a few unlucky travelers lost their way in blizzards, their frozen corpses later found within only a mile or two of their destinations. He guessed that they had already ridden for more than three hours. They should have reached Amherstburg by now. The snow fell heavily, collecting on their shoulders and arms. It was already up to his horse's fetlocks, and all the animals were having difficulty keeping their footing.

Billy rode on by himself, journeying through the darkness on faith alone. He could hear the trappers behind him, their voices growing fainter as he forged ahead. *They can stay behind and freeze if they want*, he thought. *I may be wrong, but I'm going to try.*

A moment later, he heard the Frenchmen following him. But once more their angry voices broke over the roar of the blizzard. *"Allez-vous-en!"* one shouted. The other answered with a torrent of curses. Billy turned and saw their breath as puffs of white like rifle fire in the darkness. He felt certain that at any moment they would dismount and settle the disagreement with weapons. He would not stay here to watch. "Come here, boy," one shouted to him.

"I'm going ahead," Billy called. Was his mind playing tricks? Were they planning to harm him? He urged Kumari onward.

Suddenly he saw a light flicker in the distance. Half-obscured by the thickly falling snow, the lantern-lit window of a blockhouse glowed like a signal fire in the cold darkness.

"Voilà la palissade!" Billy cried out in French over their shouting. He pointed to the wall surrounding the town. *"Allons.* Come on."

The Frenchmen fell silent. They had not known this boy could speak their language. Billy had said little to them earlier and had spoken only when they spoke English. Père Jean-Paul had not mentioned that his student was familiar with any other language. They looked at each other dumbfounded.

"Messieurs," Billy said, "we have reached our destination."

The voyageurs decided the boy was harmless after all and laughed crudely. They became almost giddy with relief now that the danger had passed. The trio trotted their horses toward the settlement.

The sentry, watching from the gate tower, lifted his rifle and called out a challenge when he heard them.

"It is I," Billy shouted over the wind, *"Billy Calder, son of Captain Calder."*

The sentry shouted to men below, and the heavy gate swung open. A guard lifted a lantern high, and after studying the travelers' faces, welcomed them. *"Au revoir,"* Billy called, but the Frenchmen ignored him. They were already quarreling over some new subject as they made their way to the home of a merchant they knew.

Billy didn't enter the town. His father had built a private home on the river beyond the palisaded walls, and it was here he had instructed his son to come. Billy reached the home within minutes and stabled Kumari, relieved that he still had the treasured mare. His father had already seen to it that there was hay, water, and a blanket for the animal.

Billy then raced across the dark snow-covered yard toward his father's house. How he longed to see his parents. He had imagined this happy homecoming so many times. They would embrace him, and give him a mug of steaming tea, and then they would all sit on the bench before the fire and talk softly.

But as Billy opened the heavy oak door, a plate flew through the air, and his mother was shouting most heatedly in Mohawk.

2 · A Straight Tree Rooted in Two Worlds

*C*aptain Calder ducked. He was a lifelong military man and knew when swift action was called for. The plate smashed against the wall behind him.

Billy's heart sank as the scene unfolded before him. His mother's voice was high and strained. She had abandoned the little English she knew, reverting to her native Mohawk. This was Billy's language, too, the only tongue he had spoken until he was seven years old. But even Billy did not recognize his mother's words at first. During the eight years he had been in his father's care, he had grown more accustomed to English.

Tiny shards of pottery rocked on the wooden floor.

Billy, who had been prepared to shout, "I'm home!" said nothing. He stood rooted to the spot, unable to speak.

Captain Calder straightened to his full height. A wide grin broke over his face as he strode to the door and shut it behind Billy. "Ah, our boy is here!" he said happily in his Irish brogue. He wrapped Billy in a bone-crushing hug. Finally Billy's mother looked at her son, the boy she had not seen for two years, and her face softened with joy at his safe arrival.

Billy glanced around his father's home, which was spacious but sparsely furnished. Two pewter candlesticks rested on the table. The twin flames and the glow of the fire lit the room. Four hard-backed chairs lined the table. A British Brown Bess musket with polished brass trim was mounted above the hearth, and Captain Calder's fiddle, which he'd brought with him from Ireland, was propped on a chair in the corner. A hall led to bedrooms at the rear of the house. Everything was neat and orderly in a military way.

"Do not mind your mother," Captain Calder said. He smiled, and the cleft in his chin deepened. "She is out of humor," he added as an explanation.

Captain Calder went to her, and she allowed him to take her in his arms. Looking over her head, he said to Billy, "Your mother is not so much angry as worried." He lifted her chin and looked down into her eyes. "Windswept Water, your stew smells delicious. The lad's made his way through a blizzard to see us, and he must be hungry."

Billy pulled off his cap and fumbled at his coat buttons with numb fingers. Windswept Water unbuttoned Billy's coat for him and hung it on a peg next to his father's military greatcoat. She examined Billy's hands for frostbite, rubbing them briskly to help the warmth return to his fingertips. She drew a chair to the fire and had him sit so she could remove his boots and the scratchy woolen socks. His feet were so cold he flinched. Her hands felt like fire to him. That was a good sign. Had the pain passed or had whitish patches covered his skin, it would have meant calling the medicine man with his ointments, perhaps even the surgeon with his knife.

Windswept Water seemed pleased. She swung the kettle

from the hearth and ladled three bowls of stew. Untying the cloth wrappings from a loaf of corn bread, she brought it to the table.

"Your mother is afraid there will be more fighting with the Americans. She would prefer that I resign from the British Army," Captain Calder said.

Billy knew his father would never do that.

When the boy came to the table, his mother finally spoke. It was not her way to blurt out greetings immediately, even with close family members.

"Straight Tree, you are as tall as Captain Calder," she said gently.

She always called her son by the Mohawk name he'd been given a few days after his birth, and she referred to Billy's father by the same title his men used.

Billy grinned. He *was* nearly as tall as his father. "*Dogéh se' gyeó óh*—I suppose it's true," he said, the Mohawk words coming back to him.

"Straight Tree . . . he is tall, is he not, Captain Calder?" Billy's mother repeated, as if she was eager to turn the conversation away from warfare. She spoke English in a soft, high-pitched voice with little chirps and clicks like a bird. Her eyes glistened with pride in the boy she had not seen for so long.

"Aye, he is a fine-looking lad, indeed," Captain Calder said. "He has your features," he added, noting Billy's high cheekbones and almond-shaped eyes.

"But his eyes are the color of the sky, like yours," Windswept Water said as she took her place at the table.

The warm smell of his mother's stew filled Billy's head. He waited impatiently as Captain Calder said grace, thanking God for his son's safe journey.

Billy and his father ate their stew with spoons while Windswept Water used her bread as a sop in Indian fashion. Billy felt self-conscious. He knew he had changed much since the time he had lived with his mother. His parents had met when his father had been posted near Niagara Falls. Later, when Billy was old enough to leave his mother's side, she had brought her son here at Captain Calder's request to be educated in the ways of the white men. And although their love was deep and true, Billy's parents preferred to live among their own people, visiting each other occasionally when they could.

His mother, sensing Billy's unease, said, "It is good. You eat only like the British now. I am Mohawk. Your father is Irish. You have your feet in two different worlds. You need to know the ways of both."

Captain Calder laughed. "And don't forget he's spent the last eight years with French Jesuit teachers."

Billy added, "And in Detroit there are Shawnee, Miami, Huron, Wyandot, and Potawatomi, all with their own customs and beliefs."

"And the Americans," Captain Calder added grimly.

Windswept Water lowered her eyes. Two of her brothers had been killed by Americans.

Billy's spoon stopped halfway to his mouth. "Father, we hear rumors about the Americans all the time. Some townspeople are saying they may cross the river into British Canada. Will the King defend Canada? Will you be called up for battle again?"

Captain Calder lifted his mug of ale and washed down a bite of dry corn bread. "You and your mother are thinking the same thoughts," he said. "Years ago, when the American armies first marched north of the Ohio River, the Indians easily defeated them. But things are different now. The Americans are pouring into the Northwest Territory, and they want nothing more than to open the area for settlement. They are clever and courageous, and they learned how to fight in the wilderness. Now the Americans want all of the lake country. It is fertile, with many rivers and streams. Timber is plentiful. It will make good farmland."

"Everywhere the Americans go, the Indians lose their land," Windswept Water said, clicking her tongue.

Billy knew his mother was heartsick since leaving her tribal home in the land the Americans called New York. When the colonists had burned her people's fields and chopped down their orchards, she had fled to the north side of Lake Erie, where she lived in a village of refugees near Niagara Falls. But she was more deeply saddened by all the bloodshed. She was tired of seeing death. She urged Billy's father to fight no more. "It is better to move," she'd said.

"I don't know what will happen," Captain Calder said. "If the Americans push too much, there may be war." He poked through his stew to find a hunk of venison.

"Father, when may I enlist?" Billy asked.

"When you are a man you may take up arms."

By that, he meant when Billy turned eighteen—an eternity away.

"That will be too late to help the Indians," Billy said in frustration.

After glancing at Windswept Water, Captain Calder glared at his son. He said he wanted to hear no more such talk tonight. Billy guessed that his father would prefer to avoid any more flying plates. He changed the subject and told of his studies while his parents nodded approvingly. He had done well during the last term.

"I can speak some Greek and Latin now, and I earned high marks in French. I know some Shawnee and Potawatomi words, too. Père Jean-Paul buys game from their hunters." His parents laughed when he described the surprise of the fur trappers when they learned that he knew their language.

Captain Calder approved. "A man who can translate will always find work in a country like this. What of your other subjects?"

"I'm studying logic and arithmetic, and I'm learning how to draw maps."

"Straight Tree, this is good," his mother said, "but do not forget the ways of my people."

"I will never forget, Mother," Billy said.

She seemed pleased when he said he'd been invited to join a fall hunting party with some of the young Potawatomi men.

After dinner, they moved their chairs to face the fireplace. Billy stared into the glowing embers of the logs. The flames jumped and licked the stones of the chimney. Soon the fire grew hot on his skin and made his eyes water. The blizzard continued to rage beyond the safety of their hearth, and the wind howled almost without ceasing. Their talk turned to the news around Fort Malden, of the military men who'd been promoted or given new assignments at other forts.

But the conversation was suddenly broken by a furious pounding at the door and a shout muffled by the storm. Captain Calder tensed and the muscles in his jaw quivered. Murders had been committed by both Indians and Americans during the past months, and everyone was wary. The pounding continued. At his father's nod, Billy leaped to the door while William Calder grabbed his musket, which was always kept primed and loaded. He aimed, sighting down the barrel of the Brown Bess. Billy slid back the bolt and watched in awe as a powerful man burst in, apparently unafraid. The stranger brazenly strode into the room, shaking the first snow of the season from his buffalo robe. His face was frozen into a harsh frown. As Billy shut the door, the man glanced at him dismissively, then turned his attention to Captain Calder. He eyed Billy's father and grunted.

3 · THE MEDICINE BAG HAS LOST ITS POWER

C hief Tecumseh!" Captain Calder cried in delight. He lowered his musket and laughed. "Welcome!" He took the visitor's buffalo robe and hung it on a peg.

With fingers stiffened by the cold, the warrior chief unstrapped the laces of his moose-hide boots and slid them off, revealing ankle-high moccasins stuffed with grass for warmth. His doeskin leggings, light as cream, were adorned with fringe along the side seam. A long hunting shirt, of the same light color and style, hung to his knees. Billy had been mesmerized by the man's gaze, which had fallen upon him so briefly. The stranger's wide-set eyes practically sparked with intensity, as though his whole being might burst into flame at any moment.

"Come sit by the fire and warm yourself," Captain Calder said. "How many years has it been? Look, darlin'," he said excitedly to Windswept Water, "and Billy . . . Shake hands, son. I want you to meet the Shawnee chief Tecumseh. His people call him the Panther Passing Across. He honors us with a visit."

Windswept Water eyed the visitor warily, but Billy, following his father's cue, pulled another chair to the hearth.

The warrior sat.

"Have you come all the way from your village in Indiana Territory?" Captain Calder asked.

"No, I have been on a journey elsewhere," he said, rubbing his hands briskly to warm them. "I cannot stay long. I must speak with you, then I go on to the Indian village near Fort Malden."

"You cannot get there tonight," Captain Calder said. "Stay with us and set out in the morning if this storm clears."

"No, there is a council I must attend. Red men of many nations will be there."

"A council?" Billy asked, hoping the warrior would say more.

The man looked at Billy again, this time with more interest. He seemed to note the boy's jet-black hair and almond-shaped eyes, and then his gaze moved to the full-blooded Indian woman who stood nearby. Finally he turned back to Captain Calder. "I have come to learn what is in the hearts of the Redcoats. I must know so I can advise my people. You and I will talk. Then I must go to my people."

"Something troubles you," Captain Calder said.

"We have let the days slip through our fingers for too long," Tecumseh said. "And with each passing moon, Harrison takes more of our land. You know that he is determined to seize all of our hunting grounds."

Billy hung on each word the man uttered. He knew that William Henry Harrison, governor of the Indiana Territory, was the most ambitious American soldier and politician in these parts.

The firelight from the hearth glinted in Tecumseh's eyes. His skin, which was tan and smooth as a hazelnut, glowed with emotion. His strong jaw was set like a rock.

"You have been a friend to the Indians," Tecumseh said. "You have spoken the straight word to us. Show me now what is in your heart, and then I will leave."

"Look at my family," Captain Calder said. "My heart is with the Indians. What else do you need to know?"

"I need to know if the Great Father of the English will help us."

Billy could see his mother's hands shaking. "Chief Tecumseh, you are planning war!" she accused him.

Tecumseh looked into her eyes. They all knew it was the women, the mothers, who bore the greatest responsibility of caring for others, who watched with broken hearts as children slowly starved to death, or who prepared the bodies of their slain warrior sons for burial.

"War is our only hope," he said. "If we do nothing, the Americans will take our land, and we will starve."

She slowly shook her head.

"Mother, what's wrong?" Billy asked, moving to her side.

"I have no more brothers to bury. I have only my son and the father of my son," she said, indicating the last of her family. "Are you asking them to go to war?" she said to Tecumseh.

Tecumseh answered, "If your husband and your son go to war, it is because they love you. Would they be men if they did nothing?"

Windswept Water mastered her emotions. Quietly she answered, "Captain Calder and Straight Tree are men."

The Shawnee chief turned back to the Irishman. "Will they help us?"

But before Captain Calder could answer, a blast of wind rattled the door, and everyone was made aware again of the terrible blizzard.

"Chief Tecumseh," Windswept Water said softly, her hands together in an imploring gesture, "stay with us tonight. The other women will laugh at me if they learn you refused my family's hospitality. You must be hungry, and we have food. You're weary from your travels. We will make a bed for you. If it pleases you, I will ask my husband to play the fiddle he brought from across the great sea."

Tecumseh relented. It would be considered rude to refuse her offer. Among his Shawnee people, women were treated with respect. A man's family line was traced from his mother's side, and it was the women who owned the fields and crops. He had not come to offend the wife of a Redcoat officer.

The council would last for several days, Tecumseh finally said. Perhaps he could leave here in the morning as Captain Calder suggested. Windswept Water ladled a bowl of stew for him. He sat by their fire and ate. During the next hour, he and Captain Calder spoke of the goals they shared.

"And so I have come to seek your help," Tecumseh said. "I need to learn what is in the hearts of the Redcoat leaders. Long ago, our chiefs were saddened when the Redcoats sent so few warriors to help us at Fallen Timbers."

Billy knew that two years before he'd been born, the Americans began to take steps to seize Ohio. His father had told him a hundred times. The Indians watched and waited while General Anthony Wayne built forts and drilled his men. The Shawnee scouts returned with tales of a colossal army, well equipped with good rifles. The Americans had many more soldiers than the Shawnee could muster, so the chiefs sent messengers to the Illinois and Indiana country with wampum belts of war urging the tribes there to come.

Captain Calder wedged another log on the grate and stretched his long legs out before the fire.

"Winter passed," he said, and Billy realized he'd begun telling the story again. "And when the time came to plant the corn, Blue Jacket of the Shawnee was chosen to lead the combined forces of the Shawnee, the Miami, the Ottawa, the Ojibwa, and the Potawatomi. But General Wayne refused to leave his fort at Greenville. He knew it would be impossible for Blue Jacket to keep his warriors from drifting away if they were kept idle for weeks at a time, waiting for the day of battle. So he stalled until late summer, when the corn stood shoulder-high in the fields. Just as he foresaw, many of the warriors grew restless and returned to their homes. When the Indian force had dwindled, Wayne marched out of his fort with almost four thousand men."

Four thousand men . . . That was an incredible army to field in the wilderness.

Even though he had heard this tale before, Billy said, "That's hard to believe."

"This American often did the unexpected. Perhaps that is why his own men called him Mad Anthony," Tecumseh offered.

"They poured forth, burning everything in their path . . . acres and acres of corn nearly ready to be harvested," Captain Calder said.

"The Miami people suffered. Their food was destroyed," Windswept Water said, shaking her head. "Their babies cried from hunger that winter. Many died."

Billy remembered the half-starved little boy he'd seen earlier that day.

"As the Americans marched north, the Indians sent word to

us," his father said, "begging for reinforcements to protect their land."

A log shifted in the fireplace, and a shower of sparks rose up the chimney.

"And you were sent," Billy said, watching the flames dance again.

"At first my commanding officers said no. Although we are allied with many of the Indian nations, King George was no longer at war with the United States. My superiors did not wish to risk a confrontation with the Americans. Finally I convinced them to allow me to take fifty of my men disguised as braves."

"To Fallen Timbers."

Captain Calder nodded. "Blue Jacket chose a place near the Maumee River where a tornado had uprooted many trees. The tangle of branches gave us good cover and made it difficult for the Americans to use their cavalry. When the Shawnee scouts reported that Wayne was within a day's march, the warriors expected combat on the next day. They painted their faces and began their pre-battle fast. They were eager to fight. But again General Wayne sat smugly in the shade of his tent. For two full days we waited, while the Indians grew weak with hunger."

"The waiting must have been awful."

"Aye, Billy, our nerves were ready to snap," his father admitted. "It was hot as Satan's hooves that summer, and the whine of the cicadas droned in our ears all day long. The sky was heavy with clouds, but not a breath of air. Then on the third evening it suddenly grew dark, and a cool wind turned the leaves. Thunder and lightning split the sky. Pouring rain drenched us as we crouched among the fallen trees throughout the night.

"When dawn broke, the men were sorely disheartened to

know that Wayne and his men had remained dry in their tents, while we were wet to the bone and light-headed with hunger. Blue Jacket sent a third of his warriors to bring food, and that was when Wayne attacked." Captain Calder spoke with grudging admiration for the American who had outsmarted all of them.

"We heard the *rat-a-tat* of their drums as they marched upon us, and we knew it was time. At Blue Jacket's war cry, the first shots were fired. At one point, the Americans retreated before us, but then we heard Wayne's voice booming over the battlefield as he whipped his men back into line. For months he'd been drilling his soldiers, and they quickly regrouped. Facing an army with twice our numbers, we had no choice but to fall back."

Billy watched his father lean forward, staring into the flames as though mesmerized by the memory.

"An eerie silence fell over the woods," he continued, "broken only by the sound of rain dripping from the leaves. Through the smoke, we saw the Americans put away their powder horns and fix bayonets to their rifles. With a *tantara* of bugles and pounding of drums, they charged, hollering their blasted Kentucky war cries. The Indians fought stubbornly, dodging from tree to tree, climbing nimbly through the branches, turning and firing, then falling back, grappling in hand-to-hand combat. But we were soon overwhelmed."

He shifted restlessly in his chair as though coming out from under a spell.

"It was over in less than an hour," he said, sighing. "That year we were defeated on the battlefield, and the next year we were defeated at the council table. The Greenville Treaty took most of Ohio from the Indians."

During the telling, Billy forgot the blizzard raging outside and imagined himself at his father's side on that steamy August day. His heart burned within him. He couldn't bear the thought of this wild country, overpowering in its beauty, being handed over to the Americans, to be cut up and divided into tidy little farms. This was the land of proud tribes—his people. It made him furious to think of the valiant Shawnee and Miami being run off from their own villages. He would fight and help the Indians regain their land.

"Father, the Frenchmen with whom I traveled said the Americans are determined to take this country. They have steadily pushed the Indians westward. There must be some way the Indians can return to their homes."

"There is only one way the Indians will ever regain their land . . ."

"They must band together," Tecumseh said. "That is the only way."

Captain Calder shook his head. "The scope of that mission is beyond the strength of any one man."

"The first steps have already been taken," Tecumseh said. "I have established a village at Tippecanoe in the Indiana Territory. It is a town open to warriors of all nations. I have begun to forge friendships with the chiefs of many tribes. This is the seed from which a great tree will grow. Now I need to know if the Redcoats will be our friends."

"Of course the Redcoats will help. Won't they, Father?" Billy asked.

"The Great Father of the Redcoats abandoned us at Fallen Timbers," Tecumseh said.

The color rose in Captain Calder's cheeks. When the Battle of Fallen Timbers was going against the Indians, they were forced to retreat to the nearby British fort with the Americans hot on their heels. There the gates had been closed against them. He recalled with embarrassment and anger the words of the fort commander from the ramparts as he and his men and the Indians had pounded on the stockade for refuge: *I am not authorized to give you entry.*

Captain Calder and his men and the Indians had dispersed into the nearby woods in desperation only moments before the American cavalry galloped their horses into the clearing. With the British watching helplessly from the parapet, Wayne had haughtily insulted their commander, then burned all of the surrounding buildings outside the walls of the fort.

"I can't believe the British in the fort refused to fire a single shot," Billy said disgustedly.

Captain Calder sighed. "The commander was under strict orders to do nothing that might provoke a war with the United States at that time."

Tecumseh spoke again, and this time a deeper heaviness filled his voice. "Among the Indians it is said that the Redcoats dropped the chain of friendship that day. It is said that they no longer speak the truth. We had thought with your help we would get our land back. But now, it seems, we are all alone. Some of the Indian leaders are very disheartened. Many say the medicine in our bags has lost its power. They say the Great Spirit has turned his face from us and that it is useless to fight any longer. But as long as there is breath in my body, I will not give up. We must stop the Long Knives before they cut down all the trees and build fences around the land, before they plow up the bones of our ancestors. We will not talk peace while the Americans are rafting their boats down the Ohio River. We must stand firm. We must let our rifles and arrows speak to the Americans."

"Tecumseh, you are not alone. Tell your people that the

Great Father of the British has had a change of heart. He has grasped the chain of friendship that he dropped so long ago," Captain Calder said. "My commanding officers know of my connection to the Indians." He nodded toward Windswept Water. "They have charged me with the task of telling the Shawnee, and the Miami, and the Wyandot, and all the other tribes, that we must be as brothers again. Together we can throw back the Americans."

Billy studied the faces around him. His mother had said little, but he guessed from the pinched expression on her face that her thoughts were with the Indian women and their hungry children. It was the women who planted, weeded, and harvested the huge gardens. Billy knew the Miami women still called Wayne *Alemfinwa*—Wind. To them it must have seemed as if a tornado had swept across their land. How they must have wept to see the fruits of their hard work destroyed. Tecumseh was still scowling as he had been while describing the plight of the tribes. There was no doubt about his feelings. He had fought before and was ready to do so again. Captain Calder's sorrowful gaze fell upon the hearth, and the firelight flickered across his grim features. His eyes glistened, and Billy was unsure whether it was from the heat of the fire or from the strong emotions he felt. He knew that his father, too, had suffered the pain of separation from his homeland.

Billy made up his mind. His heart had leaped with admiration for the Shawnee chieftain who refused to jump when the Americans snapped their fingers. He would join Tecumseh. He would help recapture the Ohio homelands.

"If it is your wish," Captain Calder said, "my son will accompany you to the Indian village in the morning should the weather clear." It was as if his father had read Billy's thoughts.

Before Tecumseh could answer, Windswept Water cried out, "Captain Calder, you must not. Straight Tree is too young. He—"

"Our son has the skills to translate. Attending a council will be good training for him."

"I can do this, Mother," Billy insisted.

The storm continued to roar outside, and the heavy door rattled on its hinges. When it quieted, Billy could hear his own breathing and the blood pounding in his ears. What if his mother talked his father out of this?

Captain Calder mused. "It would be good for Billy to hear Tecumseh speak before his people."

Then, perhaps in an attempt to avoid discord, the visitor suddenly asked to hear the music that came from far away.

Pleased, Captain Calder picked up his fiddle and bow. "Shall it be 'Barbara Allen'?" he asked.

"Yes," Billy said quickly. "That's my favorite ballad."

Captain Calder tuned his fiddle, and in a tenor voice, he began to sing:

> *It came upon a Martinmas day*
> *When the green leaves were a-fallin'*
> *That Sir John Graham of the West Country*
> *Fell in love with Barbara Allen.*

> *He sent his man down through the town*
> *To the place where she was dwellin':*
> *"O haste and come to my master dear,*
> *If you be Barbara Allen."*

O slowly, slowly rose she up,
To the place where he was lyin',
And when she drew the curtain by:
"Young man, I think you're dyin'."

"O it's I'm sick, and very, very sick,
And 'tis all for Barbara Allen."
"O the better for me you shall never be,
Though your heart's blood were a-spillin' . . ."

Billy had been watching their guest's face, and it was clear from the bemused look on Tecumseh's features that he had never before heard such music. A Shawnee warrior of his experience would have heard the drum tattoo of a military regiment on the parade ground, or as it marched into battle, but not the sentimental love songs popular in the barracks and taverns. How odd his father's music must sound to Tecumseh, Billy thought. Captain Calder would play a few bars of music, his elbow pumping up and down as the fiddle bow slid over the strings. Then he'd lower his bow and sing a stanza or two. Billy had been tapping his foot in time to the music. His mother sat quietly, listening to the mournful words of the song.

After a while, the warrior seemed to relax. It made the boy wonder about his own heritage. Was he lucky to have such parents who were so very different from each other? Sometimes he thought so, but other times he believed he was like neither of them. Lately, he had felt more and more confused.

When the song ended, Tecumseh said, "This warrior died because a woman scorned him?"

"Aye," Captain Calder answered, pleased that Tecumseh had

listened attentively to the lyrics. "The poor man's heart was broken."

"His heart was broken," Tecumseh repeated. "These words I don't understand. This would not happen to a Shawnee. Our hearts are strong."

Captain Calder appeared at a loss to explain.

"Chief Tecumseh," Billy said after a moment, "I think that what my father means is that the harmony left this man's spirit. Perhaps he was so distressed he lay down with his head to the west." Billy had heard that the Shawnee never slept with their heads to the west, that doing so would bring very bad luck. Only the dead were buried this way.

Tecumseh thought this over. "Yes," he finally said, "it must have been as you say."

Captain Calder clapped Billy affectionately on the shoulder. "You've a good way with words, son."

"I will tell you a story," Tecumseh said, "about Shawnee hearts."

Captain Calder laid his fiddle on the chair and took his place by the hearth so that the little group formed a semicircle around the flames.

Tecumseh began his tale. "The Great Spirit created the first Indians. He formed their bones and muscles. He gave them legs and feet, and arms and hands."

His voice seemed like a murmuring breeze, and Billy found himself falling under its spell. It was as if Tecumseh's whole being was given over to the telling of this tale.

"He gave them eyes with which to see and ears with which to hear. Lastly, he gave them a piece of his heart, which was good, and he mixed it with the hearts they already had, so that a part of their hearts at least would always be good."

Billy felt certain that Tecumseh spoke with the same intensity that he must have fought with at Fallen Timbers. It was a complete concentration, like a ray of sunlight sparking a flame through a magnifying glass.

Tecumseh seemed to be thinking of Fallen Timbers as well. After a moment, he said, "I am from the warrior clan. My ancestors whisper to me from their graves. They tell me the struggle will be hard. They say *weshecat-too-weh.*"

"What does that mean?" Captain Calder asked.

"I do not know your word for this," Tecumseh said.

They turned to Windswept Water, but she shrugged her shoulders. She spoke Mohawk, some English, and a few words of French, but no Shawnee.

Tecumseh repeated the phrase, making hand signs as he did so.

"I understand now," Billy said, watching Tecumseh's hands. "*Weshecat-too-weh* means to be brave or to be strong."

"Be brave," Tecumseh said. Then he said, "Courage, no? These words mean the same thing?"

"Yes," Billy answered. "*Weshecat-too-weh* means to be brave, to have courage."

Finally his father nodded and said, "Ah."

Billy wondered if he would end up spending his life explaining the British to the Indians, and the Indians to the British.

Soon after, Captain Calder invited Tecumseh to make himself comfortable in one of the rear bedrooms, but the chief expressed his preference for sleeping by the fire, explaining that he was more accustomed to that. Windswept Water brought a blanket, which she spread before the hearth. Tecumseh wrapped himself up in his thick buffalo robe and stretched out on the blanket. Clearly exhausted, he was asleep moments later.

Billy took the rear bedroom next to the one his parents shared. Still excited by the remarks of their visitor, he lay awake for a long time. Later, he heard the murmuring voices of his mother and father through a chink in the wall.

"Our son might run off to war. He will be in danger," Windswept Water said.

"Aye, he's bullheaded," Captain Calder conceded.

Billy wanted to call out through the darkness, "I am not!" But instead, he held his tongue.

"He needs to learn to walk all the way around a problem before he takes action," Captain Calder continued, unaware of his eavesdropping son.

"He is young. Keep him in the black robes' school," Windswept Water said. Her tone was pleading.

"Our son will be a man soon. He'll need to know how to conduct himself among both friends and enemies."

"The Americans are dangerous," Windswept Water said.

"Yes, I know."

Billy strained to hear more, but his parents said nothing further. The only sound was that of mice scurrying among the rafters, and now and then that of a great gust of wind as it roared through the town. Then he heard his mother click her tongue in the way he remembered from years before whenever she was unconvinced by an argument.

This was followed by the snap and rustle of bedclothes as his father rolled over in his quilt.

4 · THE PANTHER'S MEN AND THE KING'S MEN WILL FIGHT AGAIN

*I*n the morning, Tecumseh was gone. Billy's heart sank when he saw that the spot where the Shawnee chief had lain was bare, the borrowed blanket neatly folded and placed on a chair. When he opened the door, he saw Tecumseh's footprints in the snow. The blizzard had passed. Overhead, the sun shone in a blue sky.

"It's true, then, what they say of him," Captain Calder said, stroking his dimpled chin at the way their guest had burst in upon their lives and then seemingly vanished again, "—that he is a phantom. One day you see him on the shores of Lake Erie, the next he is on the Wabash or the great Mississippi."

"I had wanted to go with him," Billy said with disappointment.

"He is a mysterious man, Billy. He draws men to him as few others can, and yet he seems very solitary, too."

"Like a panther," Billy said thoughtfully.

While they spoke, Windswept Water busied herself with fashioning a new pair of moccasins for Billy. She had him stand upon the hide she'd brought, and measured his feet.

Then she cut and sewed the supple leather into footwear. The intricate beadwork on her own moccasins revealed her skill.

"I will stitch woodland flowers upon them so that my son will always walk in beauty."

As she was speaking, a soldier arrived from the fort with a missive for Captain Calder.

After he read it, Billy's father said to the messenger, "Tell the colonel that I'm on my way."

"Darlin', " he said to Windswept Water. There was a troubled look upon his features, and Billy watched his mother's shoulders sink at the tone of his voice. "Darlin', if I were a king of Ireland, I'd give all of my land away in exchange for a quiet winter with you. But this," he said, folding the note and tucking it in his breast pocket, "is an order from my commanding officer. It says that a farmer and his family have been murdered up toward Chatham, and it's uncertain whether it's the work of marauding Hurons or jealous neighbors. I'm to go north with a squad of men, find the perpetrators, and bring them here for justice. The colonel expects us to be away for at least six weeks."

"Among the Indians," Windswept Water cried plaintively, "it is different. If a man wishes to sit before the fire with his wife, he does so. If he wishes to go away and make war, he does so."

Captain Calder leaned down and kissed his wife's black hair. "I envy those Indian warriors, but you know it is not that way among my people. If I were to disobey my commanding officer, he could have me hanged."

As he embraced his wife, he added, "I have to meet with the colonel now. While I'm at the fort I'll make arrangements for you to travel home."

Windswept Water nodded in resignation. "Straight Tree," she said to Billy, "I will add your woodland flowers when I see you again."

After Captain Calder left to confer with his superior officers, Windswept Water wiped the tears from her eyes and said, "*Kanyen'kehaka tewatati*—let's speak Mohawk." She looked up from sewing the footwear together.

Billy was glad. Detroit was a gathering place for Indians of the Great Lakes area, but not so many Mohawk, who came from farther east. It was good to hear the sounds and words of his native tongue again. It was a beautiful language. But to Billy all tongues sounded wonderful. Sometimes he longed to know all the words in the whole world.

Later that day, Billy and his father walked with Windswept Water down to the docks where she would board a ship to take her back to her village.

"I had hoped we could be together longer," Captain Calder said. He embraced Billy's mother, heedless of the stares of some of the British officers who were walking along the wharf. There were those among the King's men who thought all Indians were savages.

"Our lives have been filled with partings," Windswept Water said. "We must accept it." Turning to Billy, she said, "Straight Tree, you are almost a man. Look to the trail and see that you stay on the straight path."

Billy knew that when she spoke of the straight path, she meant one's journey through life. A man must keep his feet on the straight path. "I will lock your words in my heart, Mother."

"Darlin', he is in good hands with the black robes," Captain Calder said.

Billy hugged his mother goodbye. Who knew if it would be another two years before he might see her again?

"May the Great Spirit be with you," she said as a final parting.

That afternoon, back at his father's home on the river, Billy dawdled restlessly. He couldn't shake the feeling of oppression that had come over him.

" 'Tis good that you are home," Captain Calder said cheerfully as he packed some belongings.

Home. What a foreign word it was to Billy. He hardly knew what it meant. He sometimes thought he would never have a home. Exile was his heritage, something bequeathed to him by his parents. His mother still longed for the home the Americans had taken from her. It seemed to him that his father was always on the move. He had left Ireland years before when he joined the King's army, and since then he had moved from fort to fort as ordered by his superiors. He had been at Fort Malden long enough to have recently built his private house at the edge of the adjoining town of Amherstburg. He stayed there when he was on leave from his military duties. But now he was recalled to duty and must pack his things for the expedition to Chatham.

Billy sat on the edge of his father's bed, taking the time to frame his words carefully.

"Father, I don't know why you say it is good that I came home. We have no home . . . not really." He folded his arms across his chest.

"You don't like this house?" Captain Calder asked, surprised.

"Father," Billy said, trying to explain, "I want a home—a homeland that no one can take from us or order us from. The

Americans are flooding the entire Northwest and Indiana terri-
tories. They're streaming westward, pushing before them the
Indians, and the French, and the British. The Shawnee are
refugees in a land they have called their own for many years.
The Miami have crowded their people onto a small parcel of
the country they used to roam freely."

Billy leaped to his feet and paced the room. "How could His
Majesty's soldiers retreat from Ohio? And Detroit, where you
once served, is now run by Americans. They've taken the forts
at Mackinac and Niagara, too. We'll never really have a home."

Captain Calder listened patiently. He, of course, remembered the day that his senior officers had surrendered, giving
orders to throw wide the gates of Fort Detroit. He had been
told to ferry their supplies and cannon across the river to
Amherstburg in British Canada. It had been the most humiliating retreat of his career. But it had happened a long time ago,
and he had learned to accept it.

"Your spleen runs high today," he said.

"How can you be so calm, Father?" Billy asked.

Captain Calder carefully placed his fiddle in its case and
packed it between two red woolen jackets. "Billy, don't forget
what the Jesuits taught you. 'And after this, our exile,' " he
quoted from his favorite prayer. "God promises us a home in
heaven, not here on earth."

"Is it evil to long for a place for ourselves—for the Miami,
for the Shawnee? Don't we deserve as much?"

"You want to help all these people?" Captain Calder asked.

"Yes."

"You're a gifted lad, and there is much you can do to help
others."

Billy took a deep breath. He was glad his father saw things his way. "I'm going to join Tecumseh, if he'll have me," he said. "I'll fight by his side to get the land back."

"You'll do no such thing, lad," his father said matter-of-factly.

"But last night you said I could translate for Tecumseh. I—I thought you'd be proud of me . . ."

"I am proud of you. But you're my son, and I'll decide what's best for you," Captain Calder said. "Translating is one thing; fighting is another. You're not ready for warfare."

He took his pistol and cleaned the inside of the barrel with a soft cloth. When he was satisfied with that, he polished the hammer, trigger, and guard.

"Sit down and listen," he commanded. "Tecumseh is a fine man. I wish you could have seen him at Fallen Timbers, racing from cover to cover, reloading his rifle faster than any other man, encouraging those around him. He was a very young man then, but he led the Shawnee like a seasoned warrior. It's good that you care about the Indians, but don't forget that you're Irish, too, and you've an education to learn there, as well. I'm proud of the book-learning you've done. You've acquired a good body of knowledge, but you're not finished yet."

Billy jumped up from the edge of the bed. "What good do all the books—"

"Hear me out, lad, and don't interrupt your father again," Captain Calder said in a tone of voice that made Billy fall silent.

"You will continue to study with the black robes. If you really want to be helpful to the Indians, if you want to help them win a homeland, you will first learn all you can of the white man's world. That way you'll have a better understanding of how treaties are written and the tricks the Americans have used against the Indians. You'll learn how to organize. You'll master the ability to negotiate. The Jesuits have books by men you've maybe not studied yet—Aristotle, and Aquinas, and Dante. You want to fight?" he asked Billy. "Fine, begin by reading Caesar."

"I'm too old to be a student!" Billy argued. He could feel a wave of heat creeping up his throat like a fever.

"You'll be a scholar for one more term, Billy. By the way, I've talked to John Kinzie, too. His business at the trading post is growing. He's agreed to interview you for a position as a clerk come springtime."

Captain Calder packed his camp kit with its ceramic shaving mug, brush, and razor into the trunk and closed the lid. "Don't fret about being a soldier," he said, looking up. "Peace on the frontier will not last long. This wilderness is overflowing with riches, and just because the Americans occupy Detroit doesn't make this land theirs. The British want the fur trade, and the Indians want their country back. There will come a day when Tecumseh's men and the King's men will once again fight side by side."

But Billy had ceased to listen. Another term! What could his father be thinking? At this very moment, Tecumseh was gathering his men, and Billy needed to be with him.

"I won't be a clerk or a schoolboy! I'm old enough to make my own decisions!" Billy shouted as he stormed from the room, slamming the heavy oak door behind him. But as he strode away, strong hands gripped him and spun him around. His father pinned him against the wall.

"No man slams a door on me." Captain Calder's voice was low and boiling with indignation. "If you want to be a soldier, you must first learn obedience. War is life and death, and 'tis the headstrong man who is the cause of unnecessary bloodshed."

Seething, Billy stared at his father through narrowed blue eyes. Why did the captain always have to treat him as if he was still a child? Billy's chest rose and fell like a bellows pump. He twisted away and left his father's house.

Outside, a blast of cold air struck him in the face. He strode angrily down the riverside path. Grabbing a stick, he began whacking at the snow-covered bushes along the way until all the birds took flight and the squirrels scampered chattering up to the treetops. He walked for one or two miles until he could no longer see any buildings or hear the hustle and bustle of Amherstburg. Dropping onto a log by the river, he let the bracing air cool his hot skin. His head was a stew of strong feelings. He couldn't think straight. He could barely see straight. Why was his father so obstinate?

The mournful cry of gulls distracted him. A flock of several hundred swept through the sky. How he envied them their freedom as they flew along the length of the river, searching for fish. Branches bobbed and dipped in the water as they were borne along. One gull swooped down, snatched a fish in its beak, and struggled with it back to the shore.

Billy made up his mind. Maybe not today, but someday soon he was going to Tecumseh's village at Tippecanoe, even if he had to ride between two conniving fur trappers the whole way there.

5 · *AD MAJOREM DEI GLORIAM*

"For the greater glory of God."
—Jesuit motto

*S*omething troubles you, *non*?" Père Jean-Paul asked.

Billy had returned to the boarding school in Detroit sullen and angry. And in his anger, he studied harder than he ever had before. With Père Jean-Paul to guide him through the Greek, he wrestled with *The Iliad*. Together they spoke French until Billy could converse in his teacher's native tongue as if he'd been born to it. He wrote essays using logic to support his arguments and ciphered algebraic problems until his fingers grew cramped.

During his free hours, he walked the streets of Detroit watching the Americans cautiously. Stories had been circulating about Indian atrocities on the frontier, and the Americans were tense. Every evening, all the Indians were forced to leave the walled part of the town, and the gates of the fort were closed against them. Because of this, Billy always took care to wear the clothes of a white schoolboy to avoid suspicion. But his resentment simmered. He quietly sought out some of the local Shawnee men and asked them to teach him how to ride Kumari as well as they rode their horses. He learned from them how to make himself invisible in the woods, how to build a fire quickly, and where to look for edible roots. In the woods beyond the town, he practiced his marksmanship until he could pick a nut off a branch at fifty paces. He was certain this knowledge would be more useful than reading and writing.

More snow covered the ground, melted, and then fell again as another cold spell began that lasted until the end of February. In March, when the days grew warmer and the nights stayed cold, the sap ran in the maple trees. Indian families gathered, each at their own sugar bush, to collect the sap from the trees, which would be boiled down to syrup or hard maple candy. Billy carved a deeper score on his time stick, a kind of calendar, to mark his sixteenth birthday. As the weather had grown milder, so, too, had Billy's mood.

It was the night of his birthday that Père Jean-Paul sent for Billy to come to his chambers. "Your papa sends this for you on your birthday."

Billy untied the little package. Inside was a gentleman's handkerchief of Irish linen. One corner was monogrammed with Billy's initials. His father must have ordered it from one of the seamstresses in town.

"*C'est beau,*" Père Jean-Paul said.

Within it, Captain Calder had wrapped a handful of hard candy and two oranges.

"Oranges, too!" Billy cried. What his father must have done to get his hands on these. Ashamed of his outburst the last time he had seen him, Billy said, "He is the best father in the whole world."

"Something troubles you?" Père Jean-Paul asked. "You need to see your papa?"

Billy nodded.

"Go tomorrow. I will excuse you from class."

Then, as if he had just remembered, the old man added, "I have something for you, too." The priest went to the shelf where a half-dozen volumes stood. Books were rare on the frontier, and they were jealously guarded. There were perhaps only another three dozen in the library, where the boys were permitted to read them. Père Jean-Paul took a slim volume from the shelf and turned it over to admire it before giving it to Billy. It was bound in Seville leather and stamped with gold leaf. Three scarlet ribbons trailed from the pages.

"What is this?" Billy asked.

The black robe pointed to the lettering:

Spiritual Exercises
by
Ignatius Loyola

Billy looked up questioningly.

"I have heard you say that you want to be a soldier. You know this man was a soldier. I taught you how he fought on earth in a way that made him worthy to be crowned in heaven."

When Billy opened the book, he was surprised to see that it was Père Jean-Paul's own copy. The inscription on the inside cover had been written by his mother and father long ago.

"This was given to me so that I could learn English and also to show me the path to God. You understand?"

Billy turned a few pages. Faded notes in Père Jean-Paul's cramped handwriting filled the margins of the prayer book.

"You brought this with you all the way from France?" he asked.

"It is yours now. It will help you find your way as you journey through life, as it has helped me." Père Jean-Paul momentarily took back the book. It fell open to a page marked by a ribbon, one he had evidently read often. He pointed to the words: *I must keep steadily before me what I was made for . . .*

"Billy," the priest said, pressing the book back into his student's hands earnestly. "Oh—how do you say it?" he asked in frustration. He still stumbled occasionally, at a loss for the correct English word even though he had spoken the language for years. "Each man is created for a special purpose. Sometimes we travel with companions down the same road. Sometimes the road forks and we must choose."

"I can't keep this," Billy protested. "It's yours."

The old priest closed his roughened hands over the boy's as Billy held the book. "*Non*, it is yours," he said quite firmly. "Someday you will understand why I want you to have it."

That night Billy turned the pages of the prayer book. But he was tired, and he decided he didn't need to read it now. So, after wrapping the slim volume in oilcloth to protect it, he tucked it inside the traveling satchel where he kept his few treasured belongings. He blew out his candle and burrowed beneath the cold blankets.

The next day, he returned to his father and apologized. Captain Calder, who was always ready to forgive, embraced his son and then sat down to write a letter of recommendation for Billy to give to Mr. John Kinzie. In addition to being a scholar, Billy would master the skills of a clerk.

Winter drew to a close. Finches and robins returned, and their cheerful trilling filled the woods after months of snow-muffled silence. The ground thawed. Streams and rivers flooded. And an earthy smell filled the air with a tangy richness. After the jagged mountains of ice melted from the shoreline of Lake Erie, schooners from the east reached the town with fresh food and news.

The merchants of Detroit, with their hired men, crowded the wharves awaiting their shipments of goods. Among them was a hatless man with thin chestnut-colored hair who smelled of tobacco and coffee.

6 · The Gorging Wolf Eats Our Land

I will see if he is home, sir," the maid said as Billy wiped his boots and stepped through the doorway into one of Detroit's finest homes.

Rain drove against the windows as he was ushered into John Kinzie's spacious parlor. The servant left to call the master of the house, and, finding himself alone, Billy glanced about the room. Eleanor Kinzie's silver tea service was displayed on the sideboard. And there was the upholstered sofa he'd heard about that had been brought all the way from Boston. He nervously gripped the letter of introduction his father had written Everyone in town knew Kinzie was a no-nonsense man, and Billy wondered if the merchant would, with a wave of his hand, dismiss him as inadequate.

Kinzie had started life as an apprentice silversmith. Tecumseh's people called him Shawneeawkee—Silver Man. They thought well of him. Many times when Billy had been in his store, he'd seen young braves peering into the glass-topped cases where intricately etched armbands and glittering disks made for nose or ear ornamentation lay displayed against black velvet cloth.

Billy listened to the rain beating against the windows for what seemed like forever. Finally the master of the house strode into the parlor, wiping his mouth with a linen napkin. His boots were spattered with mud from the streets of the town, and the smell of some of the goods in which he traded, coffee beans and tobacco, lingered on his coat, intensified by the humidity.

Billy introduced himself briefly.

"So you want to go into trade?" Kinzie asked after he'd read the letter from Captain Calder. "Why?"

Billy hesitated, unsure of what to say. "Actually, sir, it's my father who wants me to go into business."

Kinzie laughed. "Looks to me as if you're too honest to be a businessman."

Billy turned crimson. "What I meant to say, sir, is that I know it's an opportunity from which I might benefit, and I think I can be of service to you as well. I write with a fair hand, and I'm good with numbers. I know the ways of different peoples, and I can speak several languages."

"Which languages?"

"French, Greek and Latin, Potawatomi, Shawnee, and I still remember a good bit of my native Mohawk."

Kinzie nodded, impressed. "And your English grammar is better than that of most who are born to it," he said wryly. "What are your future plans?"

"I intend to be a soldier."

"Why? There's more money to be had in business."

"It's not money I'm interested in, sir. I want to fight."

"I wasn't aware that we were at war." Kinzie looked at Billy askance.

"Perhaps not now, but injustices can be borne only so long."

"My father was a Scotsman," Kinzie said sternly. "I was born in Canada and raised in New York. I've no time for politics. When the Americans took over Detroit, I was forced to take an oath of allegiance to them to stay in business. It's the same with my trading post in Chicago. I do business with everyone: French, Indian, American, and British. I can't afford to get involved on one side or another."

At that moment, a girl burst into the room, her dress of faded green calico swinging at her heels. "Uncle John," she called. "Oh, I'm sorry," she said when she saw Billy, "I didn't mean to interrupt."

Her eyes were almond-shaped like Billy's but of a deeper hue, like the waves of Lake Erie. Freckles lay scattered across her nose. But it was her hair that especially drew Billy's attention. Dark and wavy, it was brushed back from her face and fell nearly to her waist. A braided coronet, which Billy thought prettier than a diamond tiara, held her hair in place. Her coloring made him wonder if she might be of mixed blood, too.

Billy felt as if someone had just punched him hard in the chest. She was the most beautiful girl he'd ever seen, but she seemed completely unaware of her comeliness.

"Come in, Jane. You're not interrupting. I'd like you to meet Billy Calder. His father is an officer over at Fort Malden. Young Mr. Calder and I have finished our business."

As she drew nearer, Billy caught the scent of freshly baked bread. Patches of flour dusted her skirt. She glanced at him, and their eyes locked for an instant.

Billy stammered an awkward greeting. There were no girls at the Jesuit boarding school, and few of the British officers had their wives or daughters with them. As far as he was concerned, this amazing girl might just as well have leaped down from the stars.

"Come to my store tomorrow after your classes," Kinzie said. "I can use another clerk."

The interview was over, and against his inclination Billy departed. He'd wanted to stay and stare at this extraordinary girl called Jane. There was something about the way she moved, the way she smelled, the sound of her voice. He wanted to stay and listen to what she had to say. He'd gone to John Kinzie's house half hoping the trader would turn him down. Now he found himself excited that Kinzie had said yes.

Twice in the weeks that followed Billy saw Jane in the store, bringing lunch to her uncle in a basket. But each time she'd come and left so quickly he'd been unable to even wish her good day.

At Kinzie's trading post and under the owner's guidance, Billy learned to become a good judge of pelts, most of which were now being brought in from the country north and west of Detroit, from Mackinac and the northern lake country. He learned how to bargain with the voyageurs who paddled their canoes stacked high with beaver skins. He also arranged for goods from the east, Quebec City and Montreal, to be sold or bartered among the people of the Great Lakes area.

One evening in mid-May, John Kinzie called Billy into the office he kept in the back of his store. The smells of ink and leather mingled in the small room. Kinzie sat at his desk lit by the soft glow of the oil lamp. His ledger books lay open before him.

"Sir?" Billy asked.

Kinzie leaned back in his chair. "I need to return to Chicago

to attend to my store there. A letter arrived this morning in-
forming me that my man there died last month. My brother
will stay behind and manage this one. I'm taking my family
and my niece, Jane, and six wagons of goods to trade. Will you
drive one of the wagons?"

Chicago . . . the place of the onion fields. Of course Billy had
heard of it. A trading post at the mouth of the Chicago River
where it flowed into Lake Michigan made good sense. It was
easy to see why Kinzie was a rich man. He had first pick of the
beaver pelts brought in by voyageurs from the upper Great
Lakes. Billy was curious, too, about the tribes in the area. If he
went west, he might meet warriors from the Potawatomi, the
Sauk, the Fox, and the Ojibwa tribes. The school term had
ended, and his father had said he could make his own decisions now.

When he realized that John Kinzie was impatiently tapping
his fingers on the edge of the desk, waiting for a reply, he
hastily answered. "Yes, I'll come. It will be a privilege, sir."

A man on horseback could pack a saddlebag and ride from Detroit to Chicago in seven days if the weather was fair. But John
Kinzie was taking his family, including his wife and small children, and plenty of goods to restock his post. They would take
cattle and packhorses and enough men to guard and lead them
through the wilderness. It would be a long journey.

The days that followed were a flurry of activity, with Mr.
Kinzie entrusting Billy with more and more responsibilities.
Finally, the evening before they were to depart, the merchant
took Billy aside and reviewed his instructions. "By the way,"
he said as he was leaving, "the other men are a bit rough-

mannered. I would feel better if you drove the wagon in which Jane and my children will ride."

Billy stood alone in the deepening twilight outside the trading post, the strong scent of tobacco dissipating as his employer strode home. He was stunned by his good fortune.

For the first two days of the journey, Jane had placed a parcel between herself and Billy on the driver's bench and said very little. But on the third day, a balmy wind blew as the wagon jounced over the trail, and it seemed to lift the girl's spirits. She relaxed and spoke more openly. She admired Kumari, who was tethered to the back of the wagon for Billy's journey home. She spoke of people she had met at her uncle's store and of places she had visited.

Billy had guessed right. Her mother was of the Ojibwa tribe. Her father was John Kinzie's stepbrother, who helped manage the store. She had lived with both peoples and claimed to be as comfortable in a lodge of poles and skins as in a frame house. "It doesn't matter where you live if you're with your family," she said.

"Won't you miss Detroit?"

"The Kinzies are my family now. My home is where they dwell."

Billy told her how furious he was that the Americans had taken Detroit. "Our people need their own land," he insisted.

"The Americans are talking of war. Is that what you want?"

"I'm willing to fight to get it back."

"It might not be possible. I've talked with plenty of Americans. They'll never give up Detroit," she said. Then she changed the subject.

On the fourth day, when he asked her why she didn't live

with her mother, Jane's face darkened. She lowered her eyes and smoothed her dress over her knees.

"I'm sorry," Billy said. "I didn't mean to pry."

"It's all right," Jane said, looking up. Her eyes glistened with tears. "My mother left my father and married another man. Her new Ojibwa husband didn't want me. So she sent me back to my father. Father lives in a room above the store. He said it was impossible for him to raise a daughter, so I live with the Kinzies."

"Your Aunt Eleanor seems nice."

Jane agreed. "Yes, she's been very good to me." Then she returned to the incident, which she'd apparently kept hidden for a long time. "But why did my own mother leave me?" she asked angrily. "And now my father says it's better for me to go to the Chicago store with Aunt Eleanor than to stay behind with him. It's humiliating to be dumped on relatives." She paused again, her mood changing abruptly like a weather vane in a storm. "Someday I'll have my own family, with lots of children, and I won't send any of them away."

One of the Kinzie children crawled forward from his pallet in the back of the covered wagon. He climbed onto Jane's lap and tugged playfully at her braids. He nodded when she asked if he wanted to hear a story.

Billy glanced from the road to her face, waiting to hear what she would say. She rolled her eyes as if searching her memory for a good story. Soon her features lit up with satisfaction.

"Many, many years ago," she began, "water covered the whole earth. There were only fish and birds and animals that swam on the water's surface. One day an amazing thing happened. A woman fell from the sky. She tumbled a long, long way . . ."

The sun came out from behind a cloud, warming them.

"Look," Jane said, pointing. "She fell from a cloud just like that one."

Billy listened intently.

"A pair of loons flew up and caught her and placed her on the back of a giant turtle. The turtle said to the sea creatures, 'Bring me some mud from the bottom of the sea.' First the beaver dived. But the sea was too deep, and he failed. Then the snake dived, but he, too, failed. Finally a small toad said he would do it. All the other animals laughed at him. 'You are too small for the task,' they said. But the toad insisted. He dived into the sea. Down, down he swam. Soon the water grew very dark and very cold, but he kept going even though he thought his lungs would surely burst."

The other children stirred in the wagon, coming forward to hear Jane's story.

"At last," Jane said, "he reached the bottom of the sea. He scooped up some mud and returned to the surface. The woman took the mud and spread it upon the back of the turtle, where it grew and it grew and it grew. It grew so much that it became a great land, with trees and mountains and rivers. And that is how the world was made."

Billy drank in the sound of her lark-like voice as it rose and fell. When one of the children pressed her for another tale, he was the first to encourage her.

That evening, as he settled down to sleep at the men's end of the camp, Billy heard Jane singing a lullaby to the children. He lay on his back, nestling his head in his arms. He couldn't wait for morning to come so he could be near her again.

Despite the daily difficulty of coaxing the oxen through the woods or over the prairie or through waist-deep streams where everyone had to get out and push, Billy wished their journey might last a long time. However, a few weeks after they set out, they spotted the walls of Fort Dearborn in the distance. One side of the fort faced Lake Michigan, where sand dunes sloped down to the shore. Another side faced the mouth of the Chicago River. Sentries watched from the blockhouses, taking note of the arrival of the small wagon train. They knew John Kinzie and waved to the merchant when he announced himself. A ferry took them across the river to Kinzie's post.

That evening, Billy found himself, ledger book in hand, checking off the same inventory he'd helped to pack weeks ago as it was now unloaded. Soon the shelves in the store sagged under the weight of heavy iron kettles and axes. There were steel knives and bolts of blue and white cloth, blankets, clay pipes, silk thread, awls, and ivory combs.

A few old friends from the growing settlement came to welcome the Kinzies back.

"Things have changed while you've been away, John," one man said.

"How so?" John Kinzie asked. He draped his tired frame in a chair. Pulling his boots and stockings off, he eased his blistered feet into the steaming tub of hot water Eleanor brought in.

"The Americans are stockpiling food and weapons in the fort. They expect war to be declared against the British."

"Surely it's only a precaution. If there is fighting, it will be in the east and on the high seas," Eleanor offered.

"I don't know, Mrs. Kinzie. The chiefs in the lake country were angry when the Americans built their forts here and farther north at Mackinac."

During the week that Billy stayed to rest Kumari, John Kinzie repeatedly asked him if he might consider staying on.

"I've come to rely on you, Billy," the merchant said as he stood at the counter checking the figures Billy had just tallied. As usual, they were correct, and the young man had reckoned the totals in less time than it took Kinzie himself.

"War is coming," Billy said.

"All the more reason to stay here where it will be safe."

But Billy wouldn't listen. Earlier that day, an interesting customer had entered the store, a young Potawatomi chief with his two wives and half a dozen children. He was a burly giant, and at first glance he looked menacing. As soon as Eleanor Kinzie saw him, she retreated hastily to her kitchen. Everything about him was wide—his face, his shoulders, his chest. He had legs like tree trunks. His hair shone handsomely with bear grease, and it was cut short across his forehead, making his head appear even rounder and wider. He had come heavily armed with a knife and war club in his belt, and a rifle slung over his shoulder. But Billy knew that a man traveling with his wives and children was not looking for trouble.

"*Bozho,*" Billy said, using the Potawatomi word of greeting. "Is there something you'd like to see?"

The man strode to a table covered with a trader's blanket on which was spread every imaginable kind of personal ornamentation. He examined each item with deliberate scrutiny, and finally settled on a pair of large silver disks to be worn in his ears. After that, he allowed one wife to choose an iron cooking kettle, while the other picked out a beaded belt. For the children, who'd been squealing with delight since the moment they'd entered, he bought a bag of hard candy. He paid with some of the best pelts Billy had ever seen.

He told Billy that his name was Shabonee. He was the chief

of a small village a half day's ride away. He said he knew Kinzie by reputation, and he had come here out of curiosity. The trader was welcome, Shabonee told Billy; the Bluecoats in the fort were not. Shabonee's people had already seen Americans with their surveying equipment roaming the countryside. It was not a good sign. A few had even built cabins. Shabonee had said he was worried. He knew what had happened to the Mohawk and other tribes to the east. When he mentioned Tecumseh's name, Billy felt sure this was a man he wanted to know.

That night, Billy lay on his bunk in the barn while the other hired men played cards by the light of a lantern. A springtime storm blew through, and outside, the wind rushed through the trees. Rain pattered on the roof and dripped through the corner eaves. After an hour, the cardplayers tired of their game and stretched out on their bunks. Billy remained awake in the dark, mulling over the day's conversation. It seemed to him that there was only one course of action he could take.

Billy got up and lit the lamp on the table. He took from his satchel the pen and paper and tiny bottle of ink he kept wrapped in a cloth bundle. After pulling the stopper from the bottle, he dipped the quill pen and began to write:

Dear Father,

Why is it so hard to know what to do?

A thousand arguments stampede through my head like frenzied horses, each vying for ascendancy. School, business, a soldier's life . . . But the one that keeps leading the herd is the thought that I can no longer be idle while my Indian people lose their land.

I will tell you, Father, my blood was up when I learned the Americans have begun to settle here in the land of Illinois. Will they never be satisfied? I had thought this frontier at least would be safe from their avarice. I think they are great scoundrels for taking the hunting grounds in this country and turning them into pig farms.

I'm going to find Tecumseh before it's too late.

At that moment, one of the hired men turned restlessly in his bed and grumbled, "Put out the light, Calder!"

Billy hurriedly scrawled a closing:

> *I want you to be proud of me, Father.*
> > *Your loving son,*
> > *Billy*

Then he extinguished the lamp.

Early the next morning, Billy strode to Kinzie's house. Although the downpour had subsided, a steady drizzle still fell. Puddles lined the lanes and dotted the corrals surrounding the post. The river, running high, was gray and rippled. Beyond the water, Fort Dearborn loomed gloomily, shrouded behind a curtain of mist.

"Sir," Billy said abruptly when Kinzie himself answered his knock, "I've come to say goodbye."

"I thought you'd wait a few more days before returning to Detroit."

"I'm not returning to Detroit . . . just yet. I'm going to find Tecumseh. Will you send this letter to my father telling him I'll be delayed?"

"Yes, but . . ." Kinzie yawned, slowly taking in what Billy had said. His eyes were still swollen with sleep. The merchant, who had not yet combed his hair, was buttoning his shirt.

"Tecumseh is a warrior," he said in warning.

Everyone knew that Tecumseh was gathering braves, that sooner or later he would take the warpath.

"It's the only way," Billy said.

"Are you sure?"

Billy paused, wishing he was certain. When he was younger, he was always sure. Now he often found himself wondering if he'd make the right decision.

"Billy, you've a good future here."

"I'm grateful to you, Mr. Kinzie, but I've made up my mind."

Kinzie sighed. "In that case, I will not try to dissuade you. A man must choose his own path." He fastened his shirt cuffs and nodded toward the sound of the women's voices in the kitchen beyond the front dining room. "I am not the only one here who will miss you, though."

Billy took a deep breath. "Might I speak to Jane for a moment?"

"Yes, of course."

The trader left to get her, and presently Jane entered alone, wiping her hands on her apron.

"I'm leaving," Billy said. "I'm going to find Tecumseh."

"I know you spoke of this on our journey, but I'd hoped you would stay awhile with us." She smiled ruefully. "I feel as if I've known you forever. I finally find a friend with whom I can speak from my heart, and—" Her voice caught with disappointment, and she glanced down at the floor. "How long will you be gone?"

"I don't know. For as long as it takes to win a homeland—a place where we can live," Billy said to let her know how much he cared for her. He awkwardly took her hand. He brushed the flour from it, and they both laughed. But Jane's smile melted away and tears filled her eyes when Billy raised her hand to his lips and gently kissed it. He hated leaving her. He remembered how she had been left before, and no one had returned to get her. "I *will* come back," he promised, "when the fighting is over."

She stared into his eyes as if trying to gauge his truthfulness. Their glances locked, and Billy knew he was with the finest girl in the Northwest Territory. He kissed her hand again. Jane shyly pulled away and tucked a stray lock of dark hair behind her ear. She gazed into the distance beyond Billy where the wide Chicago River flowed into Lake Michigan. The air was rich with the scent of spring grass and wild onion.

"Do you really have to leave?" Jane asked.

"Wouldn't you like your own land—a place where you could always live and no one could order you to leave?"

"Yes, I would like a home very much," she said wistfully. "But I don't know if what you say is possible."

"Of course it's possible!" he said, his voice rising.

"Why are you so angry?" she asked.

"I've lost my home!"

"I've lost my home, too," she said, quietly.

"Well, I'm going to get it back for you."

Why did it seem, he wondered, that they were using the same words and yet speaking of two different matters?

He walked out into the rain toward the stable to get Kumari. Turning back once, he saw Jane watching him from the open door.

First he would visit Shabonee. His village was not far, and the young chieftain would likely have news of Tecumseh. The trail to the Potawatomi settlement took Billy south along the bank of the Chicago River. He rode through copses of cotton-woods and willows. Then he turned from the river and rode across the prairie under a dark, lowering sky. Rain struck him in the face and dripped from his hair. Now and then he passed small cabins. *Squatters,* Billy thought. *These Americans have no business here.* On the last rise he paused before riding down into Shabonee's village.

The settlement was quiet except for one old dog that ventured out to bark at Billy. There were only ten or fifteen dwellings, and rain had driven everyone inside. Wisps of smoke rose feebly from each smoke hole. Billy dismounted by the largest *wegiweh*, guessing it to be the chief's.

Billy called out, and when he heard a word of welcome, he entered the snug lodge crowded with women and children. It was warm within. Bunches of herbs and wild onions hung from the rafters, and several pairs of snowshoes dangled from the beams. The perimeter of the home was lined with sleeping platforms cushioned with thick furs.

"Welcome," Shabonee repeated. "It is the Sauganash we saw yesterday," he said to the women, who had looked up from their work of grinding nut meats. He called Billy by the com-monly used nickname meaning "Englishman." The elder of his two wives said, "Welcome, Sauganash."

Shabonee was sitting on a blanket near the fire fashioning a deer-antler whistle for a little girl who watched eagerly by his side. He put his work down and gave Billy his full attention.

"Can we speak?" Billy said.

Shabonee gestured for him to come and sit. He filled his pipe with a blend of dried leaves called kinnikinnick. He lit it and drew on it deeply. With his free hand, he wafted the smoke over his head. He passed the pipe to Billy, who inhaled the sweet-smelling smoke into his lungs.

They spent the afternoon listening to the rain and talking as if they were old friends.

"Harrison. You have heard of this man?" Shabonee asked.

"Yes, of course," Billy said. The Americans in Detroit spoke as if William Henry Harrison were a god. The latest stories about the governor of the Indiana Territory were of the great house on the Wabash River he had built for himself. According to the gossip, it had imported rugs and a mahogany piano and large mirrors on the walls.

"He is pushing again."

"What do you mean?"

"He pushes us from our land," Shabonee said. "He negotiates with a few chiefs who are willing to sell their country for a bottle of whiskey. He wants all of Indiana now. The Illinois country will be next."

"But the north is reserved for Indian hunting grounds," Billy protested.

Shabonee lit the pipe again, and after he exhaled the bluish smoke, he said, "He eats our land like a wolf gorging himself."

Billy mentioned the isolated cabins he had seen. "The Americans have not kept their word. The treaties are worthless."

"Bah!" Shabonee burst out. "They say the treaties are written to protect us. But treaties have not protected the red nations. I think perhaps we should change our tobacco smoke for powder smoke." Then Shabonee mentioned the name Billy had come to hear. "Tecumseh has visited me."

"Tecumseh! How is he? What are his plans?" Billy asked.

"He is well. But his younger brother stirs up trouble. Many think that he has always been a worthless scoundrel, but the Shawnee have tolerated him for Tecumseh's sake. His name was once He Who Makes a Loud Noise. One day he fell into a trance that lasted so long everyone in the village thought he was dead. When he returned to the land of the living, he claimed to have seen a vision from the spirit world. He changed his name to Tenskwatawa—The Open Door."

"The visions he sees are from whiskey," Shabonee's first wife ventured to say as she kneaded a lump of dough to make fry bread.

Shabonee nodded. "He has become a medicine man for the Shawnee and has drawn up a list of rules they are to live by. Those who disobey him he burns at the stake. When he foretold the darkening of the sun, the people believed that the Great Spirit told him. Now they call him the Prophet, and they fear his power."

Billy knew of the eclipse. He had read about it in *The Farmer's Almanack*. "It's not by magic that he made that prediction."

Shabonee warned, "*Nasana*—be careful. Do not make this man your enemy."

"I'll be careful," Billy promised. "Tell me about Tecumseh."

Shabonee leaned back and crossed his arms over his chest. "He has made Tippecanoe a town like no other. Indians of all nations are welcome."

"I want to see him."

"He is not there now."

"Where is he?" Billy asked.

Shabonee shrugged his shoulders. "With the Ojibwa," he

suggested, naming the tribe to the north. "Or the Blackfeet." This was a nation that lived far to the west. "Or maybe he is among the Cherokee in the land where it never snows."

Billy lit the pipe and inhaled the kinnikinnick as Shabonee's small children played a game of Hide the Bone in a Moccasin at his feet. Their giggling contrasted with the serious talk of their elders. As Billy exhaled a cloud of smoke and passed the pipe to his new friend, one of Shabonee's small sons launched himself playfully onto the visitor's back. Joining in the spirit of the game, Billy rose and turned this way and that, growling like a bear at the pack of children. He roared at them. He twisted and clawed the air. Shabonee's children scattered, shrieking with laughter.

Later, the oldest daughter was sent to fetch all their friends and relatives throughout the village. One after another, visitors ducked inside the *wegiweh* to visit. Shabonee's first wife presented a bowl filled with a buttery paste of ground hazelnuts. It was passed around, and each person dipped warm fry bread into the sweet mixture.

Everyone was curious about Billy. Some pointed to the moccasins on his feet, his black hair, and his high cheekbones. Others shyly reached out and touched his linen shirt, so different from their own buckskin hunting shirts.

"*Nishnabe'negin*? Are you Indian?" one man asked.

"I am *aptozi*," Billy answered, "a half-breed."

Shabonee shook his head. "This word means half a man," he said, correcting Billy. "I do not see *aptozi*, I see a whole man before me."

"*Iwgwien*—thanks," Billy said. This was a term he guessed he would use often among these friendly people.

The rest of the day was spent in laughter, storytelling, and talk of politics. Shabonee's people were determined to keep their land. They wondered about Billy's ties to the British.

"Will they help us?" they asked.

The question left Billy speechless.

7 · A Bundle of Sticks Is Strong

*T*he June sun beat down on Billy's head, warming his hair as he rode toward Tippecanoe. He had stayed with Shabonee's people for a week, pestering everyone in the village to teach him more of their language and history, as much as he could learn in a short time. But, eager to find Tecumseh, Billy had left after getting Shabonee's promise to join him in a few weeks.

Now, although it was only midmorning, the buzz of cicadas already filled the air. Kumari made a path through a prairie teeming with the tall blooms of wild rye and purple coneflowers. Clouds of grasshoppers sailed before them, while high overhead an enormous flock of passenger pigeons darkened the sky like a storm cloud. Billy stopped for a quarter hour to watch its flight.

Four days later, he reached Tecumseh's town, built where the Tippecanoe River emptied into the Wabash. Billy had never before seen such a large Indian settlement. It stretched for nearly two miles. A spacious council house dominated the center of town. On the far side of the creek, women and girls tended their gardens. He knew they'd be planting corn and pumpkin and squash from last year's seeds. His mother had once shown him how she trained bean vines to climb up the cornstalks, while she planted pumpkins and squash to spread their broad leaves over the ground to keep down weeds. At the edge of the field, a baby began to cry from the safety of his Indian cradle, a carrying device that a mother could either wear on her back or hang from a low tree limb. A woman dropped her deer-antler hoe and gently rocked the child.

Dismounting on the outskirts of the town, Billy led Kumari toward the settlement. Suddenly the placid scene was torn by the screams of terrified children. A moment later, a little boy and girl bolted toward him down the lane. They ran to Billy and clung desperately to his legs. A man, hunched over and dragging himself like a monster, chased after them. He wailed hideously. His face was twisted in a grimace calculated to frighten the children, and Billy saw that he had lost an eye in some long-ago accident. When he caught up to them, he resumed his normal posture and laughed.

"Ohh," he said to Billy with exaggerated disappointment, "you have ruined my fun." He spoke in Shawnee.

Billy saw the knife he'd been holding as he slid it back into its sheath.

"I was about to skin them. Do you think there would be enough for a nice pair of moccasins or two?"

The children dug their fingers into Billy's legs.

"You've scared them enough, it seems," Billy said in Shawnee. He muttered to himself in English, "You ought to be ashamed of yourself."

As the man lurched closer, a powerful stench filled Billy's nostrils.

Inches from Billy's face, his eyes half-closed in drunkenness, the man said, "I know the white man's tongue."

"Then I'll say it in English," Billy answered. "You stink of whiskey. Get away from here and leave these children alone."

Billy unlocked the children's grip on him. He knelt on one knee and spoke to them calmly in Shawnee. "Is your mother nearby? Yes? Go and find her."

With a last fearful glance at the monster, the children ran home.

"Trader," the man said, leaning drunkenly on Billy's shoulder. He'd taken notice of Billy's saddle and the traveling parcels still strapped to his horse. "Take your trinkets away. We don't need your beads and cloth."

"I've not come to trade. I've come to find Tecumseh."

"Tecumseh!" the man retorted. He threw his head back and laughed as if the name were a great joke. Then he shook his head. "My brother is too friendly with the whites."

He staggered away, leaving Billy staring after him in surprise.

Brother! Billy thought. *That miserable man is Tecumseh's brother?*

Later, at the House of Strangers where visitors to Tippecanoe were welcomed and lodged, Billy was given food and a gourd filled with cool water to slake his thirst. News had already spread, for someone had seen his encounter with the village medicine man.

"Stay away from him," one visiting Fox warrior whispered. "The man they call the Prophet will bring ruin."

"Why do you say that?" Billy wondered.

"In my dreams, I see him covered with the blood of his own people."

The man spoke with such conviction that Billy felt the hair on his neck prickle.

"Tecumseh cannot bring himself to drive his brother away," he added. "They say he hopes his brother will change. He is away now, and the Prophet always acts as if he is the village chief when Tecumseh is gone."

"I'll stay away from him," Billy said.

But the next day it was Tenskwatawa who sought out Billy.

Still believing Billy to be a trader, he asked, "Have you any whiskey?"

"No. Besides, I'm told that Tecumseh won't allow it in his town."

"He'll never know. He is among the Ojibwa and will not return until the sun sets two more times."

As Billy turned from him in disgust, a man's deep voice announced, "He has returned."

The sound came from the woods. Billy whirled around but saw no one. Tenskwatawa shrank back. Slowly, like a phantom taking shape, a man materialized among the trees. His commanding voice befitted the warrior who now stepped forward into the open. He stood fewer than fifteen feet from them. Yet neither Billy nor Tenskwatawa had seen him. Stunned by the man's skill at concealing himself, Billy could only stare.

The Shawnee boasted of being the handsomest of tribes, and once more Billy could see that, in this man, the claim might be true. With the exception of the strong jaw, which jutted forward slightly, giving the warrior a look of unwavering determination, his features were perfectly proportioned.

Tecumseh's eyes smoldered with indignation at what he had just witnessed. His face was grim, and the downturned lines of his mouth had hardened into a disapproving frown.

He was armed with a silver-mounted rifle. A tomahawk was tucked in his belt. Two eagle feathers trailed from the crown of his head and brushed his shoulder as he turned to speak to them. From his nose dangled three tiny crosses, similar to some of the ornamentation Billy had sold in John Kinzie's store. The man held himself like a king.

"Brother, welcome," Tenskwatawa said. When that was met by an icy silence, he began to complain. "I only wanted some whiskey. Why do you begrudge it to me?"

"Whiskey is poison," Tecumseh said, coming forward. "I see you staggering among the *wegiwehs* and I am ashamed."

"You drank."

Tecumseh turned toward Billy, and the light of recognition filled his eyes. He obviously remembered this boy from his visit to the Redcoats. "It is true," he said. "Sometimes I was a drunkard myself as a youth. But, seeing the trouble it brought, I gave it up. I am a man now. It is my privilege to protect my people. I cannot do that if I am wallowing in the dirt like a pig. Whiskey is hot in the belly for a little while; then it is gone. A man does not remember what he did when the poison was in him. I have urged my people to abstain, but as you can see, my brother persists in his disgraceful behavior."

"I will not be shamed before this *shemanese*." Tenskwatawa used the Shawnee word for a white man.

"You shame yourself," Tecumseh answered harshly. "Have you forgotten the Shawnee custom of hospitality?"

"This Englishman is not welcome," Tenskwatawa said, indicating Billy.

"*You* are not welcome!" Tecumseh bellowed. "Get away from me!"

The ill-favored medicine man slunk away, casting back one last hateful glance at Billy.

"Sauganash," Tecumseh said, calling Billy by the same nickname Shabonee had used, "Tippecanoe is my town, and you are most welcome."

"*Niaweh,*" Billy said, using the Shawnee word to express gratitude.

Tecumseh grinned with surprise, since few British troubled themselves to learn Indian languages. "I had forgotten that the son of Captain Calder spoke many tongues."

"I am the son of Windswept Water, too," Billy reminded him.

"Yes, I remember now. You speak Shawnee?"

"Yes."

"Have you come, then, with a message from our English brothers?"

"No, I have come on my own—to meet you, to be counted among your men, if you will have me."

"You are of the age to be a warrior?"

Billy hesitated. "I am old enough to know that we must act soon to reclaim our land from the Americans."

The boy was tall, but Tecumseh must have seen that he couldn't be more than sixteen winters in age.

"Can you read the black marks on paper?" Tecumseh asked.

"Yes, I have studied with the black robes."

Tecumseh nodded as if he was acquainted with the French missionaries.

A party of hunters returned just then, interrupting the conversation with whoops and hollers. Several men galloped into the clearing from the woods. They led a string of heavily laden packhorses. Tecumseh inspected the kill: four deer and a woodland buffalo. He seemed pleased and gave instructions that generous portions of meat be given to needy families. After they dispersed, he turned to Billy again and said, "Follow me."

Together they walked to the river along a tree-lined trail.

Tecumseh sat on a log by the water. He seemed eager to learn more about this newcomer to his town. But he began by apologizing for his brother's behavior. "Tenskwatawa has forgotten hospitality."

Billy shrugged.

"He is different from other men. He has a power I do not understand," Tecumseh admitted. "Sometimes the Great Spirit will send a vision to a man. Tenskwatawa believes he fell into a trance during which he was taken to our spiritual Grandmother Kokomthena, who stirs her pot by the moon."

Billy watched Tecumseh's face. The Shawnee spoke as if he didn't quite believe his brother's story.

"I don't understand," Billy said.

Tecumseh explained. "First there is the Great Spirit, and he is all-powerful."

Billy nodded.

"Then there is our Grandmother—Kokomthena. She is present to us in the shape of an old woman stirring her pot by the moon. Kokomthena rules our destinies. She weaves a great net, a *skemotah*, which unravels each night. But one day she will complete her net, and it will be dropped over the whole world. The good will be carried up to the sky. The bad will fall back to terrible suffering."

Billy nodded. This was not unlike what Père Jean-Paul had taught him about what would happen to good and evil people.

"During difficult times," Tecumseh said, "Kokomthena raises up a spiritual leader among her people, one who can lead others along the right path. My brother believes he is such a man. Some of the people are calling him the Prophet."

Tecumseh stared into the distance for a moment. "My brother has failed at many things in his life. Perhaps now he has found the right path for himself."

Billy disagreed, remembering the stories of Indian victims being burned at the stake by Tenskwatawa. But this was not why he had come to Tecumseh. Billy told of his determination to help the Indian people. Tecumseh listened intently. The youth's words seemed to touch him.

"We will light the fire in our council house tonight," Tecumseh said. "If you wish, you may sit among the young men."

That evening after the sun slipped behind the trees, Billy followed the others who were visiting the place called Tippecanoe, or sometimes Prophet's Town. They made their way to the large council house. Finding a spot among the young men near the door, Billy settled himself. From there he could hear the throaty calls of bullfrogs. The crowd grew as more and more warriors came to hear Tecumseh speak. When the war chief entered, they made room for him near the council fire. Tecumseh remained standing.

"Welcome, brothers," he said. "Be strangers no longer." Then he began to speak of the vision he held for his people and why he had summoned them to this place.

"The snows have melted too many times since I have stood in the land of my fathers. I know that the Great Spirit is calling me. I am troubled that the graves of my ancestors have been desecrated. I want to lead my people home."

Billy knew he was referring to Ohio, the land Billy's father had described as forests and rolling hills with plenty of streams. It had been a hunting ground teeming with game animals for the Indians. The Americans saw it only as potential farmland ready to be divided and tamed.

"This place is good," Tecumseh said, "but my heart aches with desire for the land of my birth." The Shawnee warrior picked up a stick from the edge of the fire and snapped it in two. "A single twig can be easily broken. The Americans defeated us because we were weak. But a bundle of twigs is strong. The time has come to gather all the Indian peoples into an unbreakable bundle."

He gathered a handful of sticks and twigs that had been stacked for the fire and tried to break it. But he couldn't. "A bundle of sticks is strong," he repeated.

"Soon I will visit other tribes. The Seventeen Fires," he said, referring to the seventeen states in the American Union, "have broken their treaty. They build their cabins upon our lands. Their pigs root among the graves of our people. I will no longer sit before my fire. The Great Spirit made me a warrior to protect my people. I will have to fight Harrison."

Billy nodded.

William Henry Harrison was a man of almost limitless military and political ambition. To further his career, he had promised the Americans he would open up the northwest frontier for settlement. In speech after speech, he had said he meant to defeat the Indians and exile any survivors to land west of the Mississippi.

"I will gather all of the tribes together into one nation." With a sweep of his arm from north to west to south, Tecumseh said, "We will ride to the Sauk and the Fox. We will walk among the Potawatomi, the Choctaw, the Cherokee, the Creek. We will journey to the country of the Sioux."

Other leaders before Tecumseh had drawn together some of the tribes, but never before had anyone had such a plan encompassing so many warriors from so many nations. Billy left the council house feeling as if his heart had been set afire.

Tecumseh held several councils over the following days. He said he would take a small party of men with him and begin by visiting the closest tribes. He would take the son of the British officer with him, he explained, to show warriors across the land that the Great Father of the English had picked up the chain of friendship. "We will carry belts of wampum to faraway councils," he said.

They left a few days later, ready for a long journey.

When they returned to Tippecanoe in July, Tecumseh's brother rushed out to meet them. They could see him from a distance waving a piece of paper in his hand. As they drew near, they heard him shouting, "Harrison says that little birds have told him you are stirring up trouble. He sends orders for you to report to him at Grouseland."

Billy took the letter from Tenskwatawa and scanned it quickly. Referring to the soldiers and the frontiersmen who would join him, Harrison had written:

Our blue coats are more numerous than you can count, and our hunting shirts are like the leaves in the forest or the grains of sand on the Wabash. Do you think the Redcoats can protect you; they are not able to protect themselves. They do not think of going to war with us. If they did, you would in a few moons see our flags wave over all the forts of Canada.

Billy, who had heard the Americans talk in Detroit and who had read their newspapers, knew that Harrison was a formidable leader. But before he would take to the battlefield, the American would wage a war of tricks. "This man is cunning," Billy said. "He will do everything he can to divide us, to frighten us into submission, and to steal our land."

"This might convince the tribes that the time is urgent," Tecumseh said. "They will see that they must act quickly."

There were other letters as well. One, carried by a trader who had passed through Chicago, was addressed to Billy. Tecumseh's sister, Star Watcher, had held it for the young man they called Sauganash.

Puzzled, Billy opened it and read it in silence. Then he took it to a quiet place and read it again and again before digging through his satchel for his own paper, pen, and bottle of ink.

Dear Jane,

How pleased I was to be the recipient of your very first letter. You say that your Aunt Eleanor is a good teacher, but I'm sure she's had an apt pupil in you. I don't know why you should have doubts about your penmanship; you write a flawless hand.

You asked about the sights I've seen since I left your uncle's trading post. Not long ago, I saw a herd of buffalo grazing on the spring grass along the river. Their numbers were so immense they filled the valley for as far as I could see. They are larger than the woodland buffalo we are more accustomed to seeing. The yearling calves stand as tall as Kumari.

During the time I've been at Tippecanoe I've met many people. There are visitors from far away. Some have traveled as long as two moons to reach this place. Once an entire village, some eighty people, arrived at this town. They say the buffalo have all disappeared from the southern part of Indiana Territory, driven off by the growing number of American settlements. The children were sickly from lack of food, and some were carried in on travois. They said that two of their elders died on the journey. It was sad to see them so weakened.

Tecumseh has made this town a place of welcome to all. I have seen him provide for the poorest of his people with food or hides. My admiration for him grows every day. He is a man like no other.

We're up against enormous odds. If it comes to war, the Americans have far more men and better guns. But I see no other road for us to take.

Please give my best wishes to Mr. and Mrs. Kinzie.

Your devoted friend,
Billy

At Tecumseh's request, Billy stayed on at Tippecanoe. He made himself useful by teaching Tecumseh more of the English tongue, which the Shawnee leader already spoke passing well. Tecumseh questioned him about the forts at Detroit and

Chicago and about the chief men among the Americans and the British. Sometimes their talks lasted long into the night.

Billy was glad to be helpful. He felt proud when Tecumseh asked him to tutor his son Cat Pouncing, and when he introduced Billy to others as his translator. During those weeks, many warriors from other nations journeyed to Tippecanoe. Among them was Shabonee, still wearing the silver earrings from John Kinzie's post in Chicago. Billy was delighted to see him.

One hot August day not long afterward, as the women weeded their gardens at Tippecanoe, Tecumseh sent word to Harrison that he would come.

"Don't do this!" Billy said. "You can't trust this man. He speaks with a double tongue."

"I *will* go," Tecumseh said calmly.

"Don't you remember Cornstalk?" Billy asked.

Cornstalk had been a revered Shawnee chief. Unarmed, and under a flag of truce, he had gone with his son, a boy about Billy's age, to an American fort in the Ohio country to talk peace. There they had been betrayed. Prodded at bayonet point into a small room, he and his son were treacherously shot to death.

"I do not forget Cornstalk," Tecumseh said. He seemed touched to have this youth, a lad barely old enough to be allowed to join a war party, remind him of Shawnee history.

"Don't go, Tecumseh," Billy pleaded. "It's too dangerous."

"I want to see this man Harrison," Tecumseh explained. "We can speak as one man to another."

"He will not hear your words."

"I will go," Tecumseh repeated. The set of his jaw told Billy that the warrior would not change his mind.

"Then I will go, too," Billy insisted, as if he alone could protect the Shawnee chief.

Tecumseh grinned. He was not so foolish as to appear before the Americans alone and unarmed. "You will go," he agreed, "along with one hundred of my warriors."

8 · I HAVE SPOKEN

One hundred warriors slid their war canoes into the Wabash River for the journey to Harrison's estate near Vincennes. Ready for the possibility of battle, the Shawnee braves had painted their faces and wore only their breechcloths of red or blue wool. They had sent their prayers to the Great Spirit and armed themselves with tomahawks, knives, and rifles. With the others, Billy shoved a vessel into the stream and clambered aboard. Paddling steadily, they sped downriver, flying along on the current. Early on the first day, they saw only herds of buffalo grazing in the distance. But as they traveled farther, they saw first one white man's cabin and then another, until soon every bend in the river revealed strangers upon their land.

On the sixth day, when they drew close to Vincennes, Tecumseh ordered them to hide their canoes in the woods. Beyond the trees they could see the great house, Grouseland, that Harrison had built for himself.

"Stay here and be watchful," Tecumseh said to his men. "I will take a few chiefs and a translator with me," he said, indicating Billy.

Proceeding on with Billy and Shabonee and several chiefs, Tecumseh approached Grouseland's fields and lawns. Soon they could see the porch of the estate, where chairs had been set out. Their arrival caused a stir among the Americans. Armed soldiers advanced to guard the house and other buildings. Their wives stood on tiptoe at a distance to get a glimpse of this Shawnee chief who was growing in fame.

Tecumseh halted a stone's throw from the porch steps, pausing in a small grove of trees. William Henry Harrison came out and waited for Tecumseh. It was clear that he wanted the Shawnee to come to him. But Tecumseh was satisfied where he was. Harrison paced. Finally, he sent an emissary to invite the Indian forward.

"I do not care to talk with a roof above us," Tecumseh answered the man. "Tell your chief I prefer the council to be held here where I stand."

When he received the message, Harrison uncrossed his arms and angrily pointed his finger in his emissary's face. Then he pointed to Tecumseh emphatically. It was clear that the governor of the Indiana Territory was not pleased. Other advisers intervened, perhaps suggesting a conciliatory approach, and finally Harrison instructed men to carry out a table and chairs from the porch and set them at the edge of the grove.

Harrison strode forward then, followed by his advisers. The armed guard was close behind. Flipping his coattails out behind him, Harrison sat in one of the chairs provided. Tecumseh remained standing but signaled for his men to be seated in a semicircle behind him.

"Listen to me well," Tecumseh explained in English. His voice carried to the edge of the crowd that had gathered. He stood tall, his shoulders squared. A pair of eagle feathers adorned his hair and bands of silver encircled his wrists. It was a hot day, and his light brown skin glistened with sweat.

"I am a Shawnee. My forefathers were warriors. Their son is a warrior."

He spoke in measured tones. He would not rush through what he had come to say.

"From them I take my only existence. From my tribe I take nothing. I have made myself what I am. And I would that I could make the red people as great as the conceptions of my own mind, when I think of the Great Spirit that rules over us all," he said, shaking his head slowly. "I would not then come to Governor Harrison to ask him to tear up the treaty. But I would say to him, 'Brother, you have the liberty to return to your own country.' "

Harrison bristled when Tecumseh addressed him as "Brother."

Tecumseh paced across the open ground, sometimes facing Harrison, sometimes facing his own men. "You wish," he said in a richly modulated voice, "to prevent the Indians from doing as we wish, to unite and let them consider their lands as the common property of the whole. You take the tribes aside and advise them not to come into this measure. You want by your distinctions of tribes, in allotting to each a particular tract of land, to make them war with each other. You never see an Indian endeavor to make the white people do this. You are continually driving the red people; at last you will drive them into the Great Lake, where they can neither stand nor walk."

The governor's long face had reddened. He clasped the arms of his chair. Close by, his soldiers stood at attention, ready and menacing.

"Since my residence at Tippecanoe," Tecumseh continued, "we have endeavored to level all distinctions, to remove village chiefs, by whom all mischiefs are done. It is they who sell the land to the Americans.

"Brother," Tecumseh said accusingly, "these lands that were sold, and the goods that were given for them, were done by only a few. In the future, we are prepared to punish those who propose to sell land to the Americans. If you continue to purchase from them, it will make war among the different tribes, and I do not know what will be the consequences among the white people. Brother, I wish you would take pity on the red people and do as I have requested. If you will not give up the land and do cross the boundary of our present settlement, it will be very hard, and produce great trouble between us."

Tecumseh listed all the grievances the Indians held against the Americans. He protested the many treaties gained by guile and the use of alcohol. He spoke of treaties broken by settlers and soldiers alike and of outrageous massacres against peaceful Indians. He spoke of Chief Cornstalk and the betrayal that had embittered Indians throughout the Ohio Valley.

"The way," he said, nearly overcome with emotion, "the only way, to stop this evil is for the red men to unite in claiming a common and equal right in the land, as it was at first, and should be now—for it was never divided but belongs to all. No tribe has the right to sell, even to each other, much less to strangers."

Here Tecumseh chuckled bitterly, for the notion was preposterous to him. "Sell a country! Why not sell the air, the great sea, as well as the earth? Did not the Great Spirit make them all for the use of his children?"

The Americans murmured among themselves. Many were impressed by his eloquence.

"Everything I have told you is the truth," Tecumseh said. "The Great Spirit has inspired me.

"Brother, I hope you will confess that you ought not to have listened to those bad birds who bring you ill news," he admonished, referring to the spies Harrison had sent to Tippecanoe.

Satisfied then that he had said what he had come to say, he concluded with the words many Indian statesmen used to close their arguments: "I have spoken."

He sat down between Billy and Shabonee.

Harrison unfolded his long legs and rose to his full height. His father had been one of the signers of the Declaration of Independence, and the son's demeanor was haughty. Blue steel flashed from his eyes. "It is ridiculous," he began contemptuously, "for you to declare that the Indians are all one people. Why then do you speak in different tongues? The land along the Wabash belongs to the Miami tribe. They decided to sell it, and they have been well paid. Tecumseh, you and your Shawnee have no business on that land—"

Before Harrison could finish, Tecumseh sprang to his feet shouting, "*You are a liar!* Everything you have said is false! The Indians have been cheated and imposed upon by you and the Seventeen Fires. Nothing you have said—before, or now at this council—can be trusted. You lie and you cheat!"

In his wrath, Tecumseh had spoken in the Shawnee language. Billy froze with horror. He felt the blood drain from his face. He had, after all, been introduced as the translator should the need arise, and in the first rush of Tecumseh's words, Harrison had glanced toward him, silently demanding an answer. Did he dare translate this into English—before the governor of the territory, before his armed soldiers? A second wave of dismay washed over him as he saw Harrison turn back to Tecumseh. The American had stiffened, his nostrils flared, and Billy saw that there was no need for a translator. It was clear to everyone present what Tecumseh thought of his adversary.

One of the officers shouted, "Bring up the guard!"

Shabonee and the other chiefs leaped to their feet and drew their weapons. They encircled Tecumseh, shielding him with their bodies. As Harrison drew his sword from its scabbard, Tecumseh shouted orders to his men hidden in the woods. They burst forward, many with their knives and tomahawks in their hands. Others were already taking up positions at the edge of the trees, aiming their rifles.

American soldiers were raising their rifles, too. Billy's heart hammered in his chest. His breathing was ragged—swift and shallow. He watched the two leaders glare at each other. It would take only the order "Fire!" on the American side, or for Tecumseh to shout the war cry, for Grouseland's lawn to explode in a violent bloodletting. Tecumseh had not come for this. He had come to speak to this man, to change his heart as he had so many others. He had not expected to be treated with such disdain. It was true, Billy imagined, that Tecumseh hated Harrison and all that he represented. But he had not come here today to make war. Billy felt certain that Harrison also regretted what had happened. A council must never be allowed to degenerate into a skirmish. It would be a terrible blot on his career.

With a few curt words, Harrison asked Tecumseh to leave. "We shall speak tomorrow when our tempers have cooled," he said.

That evening, in the camp the Indians had made on the far

side of the river, Tecumseh drew his inner circle together. "I should not have allowed my anger to drive me to speak as I did," he admitted. "The time for war has not yet come."

Billy slept little that night. He tossed and turned restlessly in his blanket. During the lonely hours of the night, he heard an owl call, and now and then the splash of a fish in the river. He had come to this council only because Tecumseh wouldn't listen to his protests. The youth had suspected from the beginning that Harrison would scoff at their entreaties and speak to them with contempt. Billy was now very certain that the American would be satisfied with nothing less than driving the Indians from their land. There would be no compromises. War would come.

"Shabonee . . . are you awake?" Billy whispered to the gigantic figure stretched out next to him.

Light from the dying fire glinted in Shabonee's eyes as he woke. "Mmmm," he answered.

"Will Tecumseh go to war soon?"

Shabonee moaned. He raised himself up and leaned on one elbow. "What?"

Billy repeated his question.

Shabonee rubbed his eyes. "He will pick up the tomahawk when he is ready."

"Do you think he'll include me among his men?" Billy asked.

"I think he likes you. You stood like a straight tree before the Long Knives today."

Billy chuckled. He had told Shabonee his Mohawk name. "Inside, I was quivering like the leaves of the cottonwood tree," he admitted. "There were so many rifles pointed at us." He rolled over on his back and stared up at the stars. "I *do* want to be a warrior for my people."

"Which people?" Shabonee asked. He knew the British wanted the fur trade.

"The Indians."

"Stay among us, then," Shabonee said in way of invitation, "and learn our ways."

Billy nodded thoughtfully. It was true. He still had so much to learn. Eight moons ago, when he had argued with his father, he had thought himself very wise. Since then, he had slowly come to know how little wisdom he truly possessed.

The next afternoon, Tecumseh met with Harrison again. Billy was not surprised to see that the American soldiers were heavily armed and tense, their numbers doubled. This time Tecumseh went forward alone with only Billy to help interpret. He had said he was sometimes unsure of his English, and there must be no misunderstanding today.

The Shawnee leader was most anxious to speak of the borders between his people and the Americans.

"This new boundary you have drawn will cause trouble between our peoples," Tecumseh said as soon as Billy concluded translating the formal opening statements. "The old line must remain," he insisted.

Billy had heard the talk in Detroit. He had read the newspaper articles. He knew that Harrison was determined to enlarge American territory by crossing into Indian lands. Now it became clear from the governor's speech that as long as the Americans felt themselves to be numerically superior and better armed, they would not hesitate to take what they wanted.

"The tribes will lose their annuities if they follow you," Harrison threatened.

Tecumseh scowled as Billy finished translating it into Shawnee. He asked that the term *annuities* be explained further. These were gifts of goods or money, Billy explained. Part of the annuities were paid in the form of alcohol. "It disgusts me to see the Americans use their cheap tricks against the Indian nations," Tecumseh said when Billy finished. "You have no right to ply the chiefs with whiskey until they are befuddled. It is forbidden by the Greenville Treaty. You must blame yourself as the cause of trouble between us and the tribes who sold the land to you." Tecumseh argued fiercely, "I want the present boundary line to continue. Should you cross it, I assure you it will be productive of bad consequences."

Tecumseh nodded for Billy to begin translating his words, while he watched Harrison's face to read any signs that might cross his features. He was answered only by Harrison's stony expression. Billy ended the talks as Tecumseh instructed him. "Governor Harrison," he said, "Chief Tecumseh desires that this disagreement be placed before the Great Chief of the Long Knives."

Harrison coolly agreed. "Yes, I will send word of your position to President Madison; however, I can assure you that the President will protect with the sword what he considers fairly bought."

"I do not wish to make war upon the United States," Tecumseh said emphatically. "I wish only that illegal purchases of Indian lands cease. Your stance forces us to ally ourselves with the British. Tell your President what is in my heart that he may know my intentions."

"I will tell the President what you have said," Harrison answered. "But I say there is not the least probability that he will accede to your terms."

"As your Great Chief is to determine the matter, I hope the Great Spirit will put enough sense in his head to induce him to direct you to give up this land."

Tecumseh put his hand on the stone head of the tomahawk that jutted from his belt. The muscles in his jaw tightened. He seemed resigned to the knowledge that none of his arguments would turn the hearts of the Americans. He looked to the east. He knew that the American President lived many days' travel toward the rising sun. He had heard that Madison was a small man, undistinguished as a public speaker, who had never commanded soldiers in battle. This seemed puzzling, for it was strength and eloquence and prowess in combat that marked a man for greatness among the Indian nations. "It is true," Tecumseh said, "that he is so far off he will not be injured by the war; he may sit in the town and drink his wine, while you and I will have to fight it out."

9 · THE VERY GROUND WILL TREMBLE

*B*illy had returned to Tippecanoe with Tecumseh and had walked among the Shawnee for over a year. He was now regarded by them as a member of their chief's inner circle. Many showed a genuine warmth for him, which Billy knew was rarely accorded to outsiders. In turn, he felt a growing fondness for the Shawnee. He had learned their myths and legends. He knew the patterns of woodland flowers the women sewed on their moccasins and pouches. He played the games of chance they loved—throwing the bones or hiding the pebble—intense guessing games that might last for days.

But there were those who followed Tenskwatawa's lead. They sneered at Billy, calling him a half-breed. "Your blood is tainted," they said. "Don't presume to speak with our young women or try to marry within our tribe." The words of these few had made Billy feel like an outsider. Yet Tecumseh often sought him out. He seemed to value Billy's opinions and encouraged him to speak his thoughts freely.

One summer afternoon, Tecumseh began talking about military strategy, explaining to Billy how he made decisions on the battlefield. They were sitting inside the Shawnee chief's comfortable *wegiweh* in Tippecanoe, where they could hear the children playing outside.

The settlement had continued to grow as word spread of Tecumseh's plans. It had become a symbol of hope as discontented Indians of many nations came to be near the fiery Shawnee warrior. Billy could walk from one end of town to the other and hear a half-dozen languages. But despite the differences in the way they spoke or dressed, the warriors were beginning to see themselves as one nation of brothers belonging to a vast land, not merely as members of this tribe or that. The Redcoats, too, sent messages of support from Canada to their "brothers" on the Wabash.

By the fire, Tecumseh's sister Star Watcher crumbled the leaves of a fragrant herb over a simmering pot of beans and wild rice flavored with a little rabbit meat. "Tell the story, brother, of how you fooled the Kentuckians who ambushed you."

Tecumseh chuckled at the memory while Billy leaned forward, eager to hear the tale.

"I was away with a small party of my men," Tecumseh began. "We had camped for the night, and I had taken the first watch. As my men slept around the fire, I heard the Long Knives creeping up on us through the woods. Their voices were many. They could see us by the light of our fire. I heard the *click . . . click . . . click* as they aimed their rifles. So I stood up slowly as though stretching and suddenly threw my buffalo robe over the fire, plunging the camp into darkness, shouting to my men as I did so. We knew those woods better than the Long Knives, and we were able to regroup away from the camp and attack our enemies. They lost many men that night. I did not lose a single warrior."

The talk made Billy reflect on their present situation. How might they use strategy to their advantage now? Cunning was needed, yes, but what they needed most was more warriors.

"You know Pontiac?" Tecumseh asked.

"Yes, of course," Billy answered.

"He put together a confederation that surprised the white soldiers," Tecumseh said with admiration. "He laid siege to Detroit and many other forts in our country."

"Little Turtle, too," Billy added.

It was Little Turtle who, in the prime of his life, had drawn more men to himself than any other warrior before him and had defeated the Americans in the Indians' greatest victory ever.

"I will do what Little Turtle and Pontiac did, and more," Tecumseh said. "I will gather war parties from every tribe and nation. We will surprise the Americans again."

"There's still fear among the tribes," Billy said. He remembered comments among Shabonee's Potawatomi. "They think the Americans are too well trained, too well supplied with rifles and cannons. Perhaps they won't come when they're needed." His thoughts trailed off.

After a while, Billy asked, "Should we go to Fort Malden first? I know you want to visit the tribes in the west and south, but if you were to go to them saying the Redcoats are our friends, that they have promised to give us food, and weapons, and soldiers . . . Surely that would help convince the tribes to join your confederation."

Tecumseh nodded. He also guessed that Billy might have other reasons, more personal and less to do with strategy, than he had admitted. "You advise this in order to see your father?" he chided good-naturedly.

Billy laughed and admitted that had been among his aims also.

"Let us do as you say," Tecumseh concluded. "Perhaps the Redcoats are ready to help us. They want the fur trade."

They left that week with a small group of warriors, and after several days on the trail they reached the outskirts of Detroit. Here Billy took his leave of the others and rode into the American-held town alone. He promised to catch up with Tecumseh in a day or two at Fort Malden across the river in British Canada. "Tell my father I'll see him soon."

Billy went directly to the mission school the black robes had built. After tethering Kumari in the yard, he searched the classrooms and chapel until he finally found his teacher in the kitchen. The priest stood at a table before a basin of water, his sleeves rolled up above his elbows, washing a small hill of potatoes and carrots.

Billy watched him for a moment from the open door. "Père Jean-Paul," he said quietly.

The French missionary looked up from his work. He had aged noticeably in the year Billy had been away, but his eyes were still young and piercing. The old man moved slowly as he came forward.

Billy dropped to his knees and asked for his teacher's blessing.

In the hour that followed, they spoke of books and the continuing work of the black robes as Père Jean-Paul's religious order reached out to the Indian nations. They healed the sick whenever they could. They brought comfort to the sorrowing. And they opened schools where they turned boys into men.

Père Jean-Paul asked, "Have you read St. Ignatius, my son?" He was speaking of the little leather-bound book he'd given Billy on his sixteenth birthday.

"I keep it with me always," Billy answered, evading the question. When Père Jean-Paul laughed and said, "Spoken like a schoolboy," Billy grinned sheepishly and hung his head.

"I *will* read it," Billy promised. "You have my word. But for now there are other things I must do."

"You still wish to serve God's Indian children, *n'est-ce pas?*" the black robe asked.

"More than anything."

"How will you serve?"

Billy chuckled. That was easy. "I will serve by fighting, of course."

"But the Americans grow stronger and more determined to have this land every day. It will be a difficult struggle."

"Tecumseh can do it."

"We have spoken of this before," Père Jean-Paul said. "You think there is only one way to serve your people. A rifle is a powerful weapon, but I know you can be more dangerous to the Americans with the voice God has given you. A man can fight without a sword or gun."

But Billy would hear none of it. "The voice of my rifle carries far."

The old man closed his eyes and spoke from memory:

"Teach me, O Lord, Your way,
and lead me on the straight road."

"I know the psalm, and I *am* on the straight road. I'm sure of it," Billy said stubbornly. "Would you have us negotiate with the Americans while little children sicken and die from hunger?" Billy answered the question for himself. "No, I've made up my mind, and I will not alter it now."

Immediately he regretted the tone he had taken. He took Père Jean-Paul's arm and led him to a chair. "Let's talk about something else. Tell me about the new mission in the north country."

That evening it was Billy who insisted upon serving the boiled vegetables and fried corn mush to the twenty or so boys who boarded at the mission school. Though he was only a few years older than most and had been their classmate only a short time ago, Billy now felt apart from them. Their preoccupation with games seemed childish to him. He had faced American soldiers. He had translated at an important council between a Shawnee chief and the governor of the Indiana Territory. He had ridden hundreds of miles from home alone. And yet, Billy felt a twinge of envy of their youthfulness.

He left the next morning, taking the roundabout way to Fort Malden. There was no need, he thought, for the American soldiers posted on the ramparts of Fort Detroit to see him crossing over the river to a fort built by their British rivals. First riding upriver along a narrow trail, Billy guided Kumari down a grassy embankment. He loosened the reins and allowed her to plunge into the water. Leaning close to her neck so that horse and rider appeared to be one creature, Billy clung to the strong mare as she swam the width of the river. Later, at the British fort, his father welcomed him with a hug.

"Father, stop. You'll break my ribs," Billy said, laughing. "How is Mother? Have you seen her recently?"

Captain Calder held his son at arm's length. The look on his face stunned Billy. "You didn't get my letter?" he asked. "I sent it to John Kinzie months ago in the hope that it would reach you."

"No. I haven't seen Mr. Kinzie in over a year."

"Come, Billy, we need to talk," Captain Calder said, releasing him.

Billy saw that his father's usual smile was gone, and his shoulders, which had once been ramrod straight, now slumped as though he carried a heavy burden. Like Père Jean-Paul, his father looked older.

They walked through the woods surrounding Fort Malden. There, in the forest, sheltered under a canopy of emerald-colored leaves, his father tenderly broke the news that Wind-swept Water had died in a smallpox epidemic. "The illness ravaged her village last spring . . . Few lived to tell of it." He shook his head sadly and began to cry. "Oh, son, she was a dar-lin' girl. I loved her so."

"Father, if only I had known . . ." Billy said. He tried to swallow over the hard lump that suddenly filled his throat. He would never again hear the chirps and clicks of his mother's voice as she argued a point or told a story. Poor Mother, he thought. Smallpox was a terrible way to die. He remembered when two schoolmates had come down with it: the vomiting and the fever, and the crying at night, and the awful red pox that pitted the face of the boy who survived. Billy blamed himself—he should have been there to hold her hand or cool her forehead. Why hadn't he gone to visit her? Suddenly his legs felt weak, and he found that he had to sit down. *I could have been a better son*, Billy thought. Captain Calder squatted by his side and placed a steadying hand on his son's shoulder.

"She walks with the saints," the captain said sadly, interrupting Billy's reverie.

Although tears slid down his cheeks, Billy smiled, knowing his mother would never have phrased it quite that way. She would have said that she was going to the land beyond the setting sun where the wind was mild and there was always good food simmering in a pot.

That night, in his father's quarters, they spoke hopefully of the future.

"Billy, you've told me of Tecumseh's plans. Do you really think he can unite the tribes?" his father asked with not a little skepticism. "This is such a grand scheme that the man has."

"Father, I have heard him speak, and I have seen the effect he has on his men. It's true, no ordinary man could unite the tribes, but Tecumseh is no ordinary man. He has a vision for the Indian nations that will lift them above their rivalries. We will be one people with our own land where we can practice our customs. We will have our own hunting grounds, which will not be cut up into little farms."

The next day Captain Calder arranged a meeting between Tecumseh and Colonel Matthew Elliott. Like Billy's father, Colonel Elliott was an Irishman in the service of the British, a man who also had sons with an Indian woman. Billy found himself drawn to the older man's warmth and exuberance. The boy listened attentively, held by the sound of Elliott's voice. The Irishman was no orator like Tecumseh, who was able to spellbind hundreds of listeners at a time. Instead, his skill seemed fitted to small groups, which he might charm with ease. Elliott's loose white hair fell to his shoulders, and his face was as wrinkled and cracked as the dried mud flats of a drought-stricken riverbed. In a thick brogue that issued from a barrel-like chest, he welcomed them heartily and introduced himself as a member of the British Indian Department, a group of men whose ties allowed them to bridge the gap between the two peoples.

"Aye, you were just a wee little baby the last time I saw you," he said to Billy. Turning to Captain Calder, he added, "He reminds me so of my own boys."

They passed the peace pipe. Tecumseh explained his goals and persuaded them of the possibility of an invincible Indian confederation. He spoke of the need for British help. Matthew Elliott listened attentively, nodding in enthusiastic agreement now and then.

They talked for over two hours.

"Chief Tecumseh," Elliott concluded, "I am authorized to offer you British friendship." He leaned across the table and took the warrior's hand, shaking it vigorously. "King George is not desirous of the Americans taking more and more territory. You will have gunpowder and rifles for your men. We will send blankets and food."

He took a quill pen, dipped it into the ink bottle before him, and began filling out requisition forms.

"Don't you worry about the British. If I've anything to say about it, they'll stand firm by your side."

The next day, as Billy brushed the burrs from Kumari's coat, his father came to the stable to bid him goodbye. "This reunion has been too short," he said, steadying the mare's head as Billy brushed from neck to flank. "Won't you stay longer?"

"I must leave, Father. Tecumseh needs me. I can speak his words to many people. I can help him . . . I can help him get our land back. I've been waiting all my life for this." Billy hung the brush on its peg on the stable wall and threw a blanket over Kumari's back. "War is coming," he said, leading the animal outside. "Harrison wants to crush us and take our hunting grounds. I won't sit by and allow that to happen."

Then, facing his horse, he planted his left foot by his mount's front hoof and sprang with a twisting motion onto Kumari's back. His father handed him his short bow and quiver of arrows, which Billy slung over his shoulder and across his chest. Then the flintlock rifle, powder horn, and pouch of lead balls were passed up to him.

Captain Calder sighed deeply. "Godspeed, son. Return soon."

Billy found Tecumseh with the band of warriors who would journey with him. At lightning speed, they rode to Tippecanoe, where Tecumseh gave stern orders to his brother to watch Governor Harrison but to take no steps against him.

"If he knows I am away, he may try to lure you into battle. This you must not do. We are not ready."

Tenskwatawa turned his head, to see his brother better with his good eye. "I will be chief at Tippecanoe while you are gone. You can trust me."

Billy reined in Kumari, who was pawing the ground restlessly. He had grave misgivings about this decision. He wished Tecumseh might reconsider. There were other men who would be better leaders in his absence. But the Shawnee chief had already mounted his black horse and was leading his elite band from the town. Billy had no choice. He urged Kumari into a gallop and followed Tecumseh and his men as they thundered away.

For days they rode through Indiana and Ohio, Kentucky and Tennessee. Pushing farther south, they visited the Choctaw and the Creek, the Cherokee and the Seminole, and many smaller tribes. At each village, Tecumseh's message was the same: The Americans would never be satisfied until the Indians were driven from the earth. They must unite and fight as brothers.

"These lands are ours," he would say. "No one has the right to remove us. The Great Spirit above has appointed this place for us, on which to light our fires, and here we will remain."

"I'm giving you a sacred wooden slab," he said at a Cherokee town. "It is encoded with a hidden message calling all the Indians on both sides of the Mississippi River to arm themselves."

Billy watched as Tecumseh held up what at first looked like an ordinary piece of red cedarwood, its size and shape similar to the wooden rulers Billy had once used in Père Jean-Paul's classroom. But then he saw that one side of the stick was carved with strange symbols.

"To any curious white settlers who might see this," Tecumseh said, "you must say these symbols are meant to guide us to a happy afterlife. But to your own warriors, you shall explain the true meaning of each carving." He pointed to the symbols as he spoke, his finger sliding along the stick. "All Indians," he said, indicating the first picture, "on both sides of the Mississippi," he added, moving his finger to the second carving, "must ride at lightning speed . . . with their weapons. Leave behind the tending of corn and the hunting of game . . . to become united . . . when the great sign of the trembling earth is given . . . so that all tribes together . . . take the land the Americans have stolen."

"How will we know the time has come for us to take the warpath?" their chief asked.

"Here is a bundle of red sticks," Tecumseh explained. "Watch the night sky for my sign. I will show you a sign that has not been seen for many years. The Great Spirit is with me, and I have the power to do this thing I speak of. After you see that sign in the sky, I will stamp my foot upon the earth and make the very ground tremble. And after that, discard one of the sticks with each new moon. When only one stick remains, then you will know it is time to make war."

Any other man delivering such orders would have been chased from their council house, but not Tecumseh. His reputation as a warrior and statesman had preceded him, and even the tribes who lived many weeks' journey away from Tippecanoe knew the man standing before them spoke the truth.

"Soon I will take up arms against the Seventeen Fires, and when I strike them a blow, you will know it. I will stamp my foot and shake the whole earth. The ground will give way from under the white man's feet, and he will mire down. I will be on firm ground, and I will kill them with my war club. In defiance of the pale-faced warriors of Ohio and Kentucky, we have traveled through these settlements, once our beloved hunting ground. From their graves our fathers reproach us as slaves and cowards. I hear them now in the wailing winds.

"Now your tomahawks have no edge; your bows and arrows were buried with your fathers. Brush from your eyes the sleep of slavery. Once more, strike for your country. This is the will of the Great Spirit who sends me to you. All of the tribes of the north are dancing the war dance. I must return to my country and my warriors near the great lakes, but soon you shall see my arm of fire streak across the sky."

Time and again, that was what Tecumseh said, and everywhere he went, he made an extraordinary impression. His words rang in their ears, and his listeners were stirred to action. Many warriors pledged to follow him when the time came. Tribes that had been enemies for generations agreed to act as brothers to keep their land.

But a few closed their ears to his message. There were those who wanted peace at any cost. After all, the Americans had not taken their land. When he met with such skepticism, Tecumseh spoke with incredible vigor in an urgent attempt to inflame his people.

"Where today are the Pequot?" he would ask them of the New England tribe. "Where are the Narragansett, the Mohican, the Pocanet, and other powerful tribes of our people? They have vanished before the avarice and oppression of the white man, as snow before the summer sun. Will we let ourselves be destroyed in our turn, without making an effort worthy of our race?"

Tecumseh would pause and look from face to face, daring any man present to answer. Then, with a powerful burst of energy, he would challenge them to kindle the courage that lay sleeping in their hearts. "Shall we, without a struggle, give up our homes, our lands, bequeathed to us by the Great Spirit? The graves of our dead and everything that is dear and sacred to us? I know you will say with me, Never! Never!

"Sleep no longer, O Choctaw and Chickasaw, in false security and delusive hopes. Will not the bones of our dead be plowed up, and their graves turned into plowed fields?"

Billy listened awestruck when Tecumseh spoke in this vein. The power of the chief's words never failed to burn within his chest. The young warriors around him whooped and shouted in enthusiastic agreement. But as he looked across the fire into the cold eyes of some of the older chiefs who sat stone-faced and who would listen to no more, he knew Tecumseh would not stay here long. There were many in the southern and western nations who had had little contact with Americans, who did not believe the Americans would take their land. It seemed inconceivable to them, and several chiefs refused to hear Tecumseh's message.

"Take the trash from your ears and listen," Tecumseh shouted when he came across these men. "The Americans are not friends to the Indians. At first they asked only for land sufficient for a *wegiweh*. Now nothing will satisfy them but the whole of our hunting grounds, from the rising to the setting sun."

The Shawnee warrior was fired with urgency to proclaim his message. He pushed his men to ride farther and farther to reach as many Indian brothers as they could.

Finally, however, four moons after they had left Tippecanoe, they began their return journey. As they rode north, Tecumseh touched the *opawaka* that hung about his neck. The stone, found during a vision quest, marked him as a warrior and helped him to commune with the spirit world. "I have done what I can for now," he said.

They continued on, never stopping for long in any one village. The weeks passed from fall to winter. The air grew colder as they left the warm south. Back through Georgia, Tennessee, and Kentucky they rode, often in silence. When they did speak, it was longingly. They were wearied with sleeping on the hard ground and eating parched corn. It would be good to reach Tippecanoe.

With Tecumseh's permission, Shabonee and Billy struck out on their own for a few days to hunt for the party.

"We'll meet up with you at the Beautiful River," Shabonee said, referring to the wide Ohio.

In the days that followed, they had good luck, together bringing down a deer.

"The men will be glad to eat fresh meat," Billy said as they stood over a white-tailed buck.

They butchered the carcass and tied portions of meat up in a tree out of the reach of wolves while they hunted farther afield. The next evening Billy brought down a second deer, a feat he had never before achieved by himself. Together, in the deepening twilight, they prayed, thanking the Great Spirit for their good fortune. Then they roasted some of the venison, the drippings sizzling over the embers of their fire, and ate their fill until their fingers were slippery with warm grease.

Suddenly, the sky, which had darkened to an inky black, lit up. Shabonee and Billy watched in speechless wonder as a greenish light streaked across the face of heaven like the swipe of a giant cat's paw.

When it had faded away, Shabonee said, "It is as Tecumseh foretold. The Great Spirit has given him this power."

Awestruck, Billy knew that this strange light had not been predicted in *The Farmer's Almanack*. He had come to believe that Tecumseh was a great man, but this occurrence was beyond any human explanation he could conceive.

"It's almost time for the tribes to begin counting the red sticks," Shabonee said. "It is his omen."

"What do you mean?"

"That streak of light is well known to the Indians. It is called the Panther Passing Across, and it might appear once or twice in a man's lifetime. Did you not know that is what *Tecumseh* means? They say this same light appeared in the sky the night he was born, that it was seen from the land of the Mohawk to the country of the Blackfeet. His entire tribe knew then that he was destined for greatness."

When they met up with the others at the Ohio River, they learned that the advance party had seen it, too.

Then something even more incredible came to pass.

One evening during the Ice Moon not long after Billy and Shabonee had rejoined Tecumseh and his band of warriors, two scouts arrived at dusk. These were trusted men Billy had seen before.

"We have been searching for you," one said to Tecumseh disconsolately.

Billy knew they brought bad news.

"Let us withdraw a little," Tecumseh said.

At first Billy was disappointed to be excluded. But as he watched the three men walk away, Shabonee explained. "It is Tecumseh's way. He will counsel with us when it is necessary."

From where he stood, Billy watched the three dark figures gradually become shadowy silhouettes in the deepening twilight. Soon he could no longer hear even the murmur of their voices. The air was cold, and Billy decided to join the other men where they were building the evening campfire. It was then that he heard a low, angry growl like the noise that comes from the throat of a wildcat when it is threatened. He turned to see Tecumseh facing the moon, his arms raised as if in supplication to Grandmother Kokomthena. The scouts had disappeared as if already sent on another journey. The Shawnee chief stamped his foot, not in uncontrolled fury but in a slow and deliberate sort of righteous anger. A moment later, Billy felt ripples under his own feet as if the ground had become an unstable liquid. It was like trying to stand in a rocking canoe. The men at the fire felt it, too. One lost his balance and fell. Their horses, picketed nearby, whinnied in fright and strained at their ropes. The churning of the earth seemed to swell as it spread in what Billy guessed to be concentric circles beyond their campground.

Shabonee, who was always ready to joke, was very serious when he said, "He has stamped his foot and made the ground tremble. Those who doubted before will doubt no longer."

Later, they learned that half the continent had trembled that night. The earthquake was so tremendous it had changed the course of the mighty Mississippi River. Herds of buffalo stampeded, and trees snapped in half as if they were twigs. It even woke the Great Father of the Americans, President Madison, as he slept in his bed in Washington, D.C. Far to the south, warriors recalled the words of Tecumseh.

Three weeks later, Tecumseh galloped his horse down the trail skirting the Wabash River. He seemed eager to reach his town. The new year of 1812 had begun, and he said that he longed to spend the cold winter months before the fire in his warm lodge. The ground had frozen, and twice the group had seen a light dusting of snow. But as they approached the last bend before Tippecanoe, Billy became aware of the unusual silence. Why could he not hear the cries and shouts of the children? Why were there no dogs barking or horses nickering to welcome them home?

The only sound to reach their ears was the forlorn *scritch, scritch* of withered cattails blowing in the wind.

10 • TIPPECANOE

When they rounded the last turn in the trail, they saw the ruins of what had once been their beloved home. Nothing remained of the splendid town except heaps of charred dwellings. Horrified, Billy reined Kumari to a halt at Tecumseh's side and studied the ghostly scene. For as far as he could see, the settlement had been leveled, its inhabitants killed or scattered.

Tecumseh's chest heaved with emotion. "The Americans have been here," he said with a bitter edge to his voice, "and for their campfires they have lit our *wegiwehs*. My scouts told me of this, but I did not believe the destruction could be so complete."

They slowly rode down the main avenue of the town, barely able to comprehend the eerie scene. To either side, the burned posts of lodges stood as stark reminders of the destruction that had occurred. Their food, stored underground in caches, had been dug up and trampled underfoot. Their meat-drying racks had been knocked down. Their herd of spirited horses had been run off. The hundreds of warriors who had been gathering here from a dozen different nations had vanished. Silence and desolation were all that was left of the town which had stood as a center of welcome to all tribes. Everything Tecumseh had worked so hard for lay in ruins.

It must have been Harrison, Billy thought angrily. *He fears Tecumseh and hopes to crush us. He's determined to redraw the boundary lines in this part of the country. He wants this land to become another star on the American flag.*

Harrison had destroyed a year's worth of food. Suddenly Billy remembered the hungry little boy bundled on his mother's back he had seen two years before in Detroit. Even if Tecumseh's people had been able to make their way to the black robe mission, there was not enough food to feed them all. More likely, they were wandering in the wilderness scraping the bark from trees in search of something to eat. Or they were dead.

Billy and Tecumseh dismounted when they reached the heart of the town. This was where Tecumseh's own *wegiweh* had stood. The great council house, the social center of the town, was a jumble of charred beams. Of Tecumseh's home, only the posts remained standing. The latticework walls, which Star Watcher had carefully crafted with mud and grass to keep out the cold, were shredded beyond repair. A ragged deerskin hide fluttered limply from a post. Billy squatted amid the ashes. He scooped up a handful and watched through tear-blurred eyes as the wind blew the particles away.

His resolve hardened.

They found Tenskwatawa at the edge of the town with the hungry and exhausted survivors of the battle. The camp was a pitiful collection of lean-to shelters and drafty *wegiwehs*. At

Tecumseh's shout, the Prophet emerged from his small dwelling, pulling a cloak of spotted weasel tails over his shoulders. A headdress of glistening black raven feathers sat low across his brow. Furious, Tecumseh leaped from the back of his horse.

"I want to hear from your own tongue what has come to pass at my Tippecanoe town," he demanded.

Tenskwatawa cowered before his brother. "It is not my fault." When Tecumseh took a step toward him, he said hurriedly, "While you were gone, our young men stole some horses from the Americans, and the Long Knife Chief used it as an excuse to march against us."

"Was it Harrison?"

"Yes, it was Harrison on his big white horse." The Prophet looked up with such a miserable expression on his ugly face that Billy almost felt sorry for him.

"Did I not warn you to avoid warfare at all costs in my absence?" Tecumseh demanded.

"When all the leaves fell from the trees, Harrison rode from Vincennes toward us with an army of a thousand men," Tenskwatawa said.

Billy knew there had been but one third that number left to defend the Tippecanoe town.

"Our scouts watched as they drew closer each day until finally we could see their campfires from Tippecanoe. Our younger warriors urged me to fight. When I prayed, the Great Spirit told me there was no need to fear our enemies. I counseled our men that the Americans' bullets would pass through them without harm. I told them to strike at night while the Americans slept."

Tenskwatawa's face was black and blue, and Billy wondered if the survivors of the battle had beaten him in retaliation for his foolish advice. He knew it was not likely that Tenskwatawa had fought in the battle himself.

"From a high rock nearby," the Prophet continued, "I watched and beat the sacred drum. Our braves knew that as long as they could hear the drumbeats, they must continue to fight."

But Tecumseh angrily cut him off. "I ordered you to avoid battle with Harrison. You were to abandon the town and flee to the woods."

Billy had never seen Tecumseh so outraged. His face was hard as flint, and fire flashed in his eyes.

"How many of my warriors have fallen in battle because of your foolishness? How many are scattered? Our food is gone, destroyed under the boots of the Americans. Our herds run off!"

"The Great Spirit told me our warriors would be safe from harm." The one-eyed medicine man adjusted his raven-feather headdress and smoothed the fur-trimmed cloak he wore. "He gave me the power to cast a spell that would render the Americans harmless, their bullets soft as rain," he said arrogantly. "I told our men the Americans would run like sheep at the first noise."

"But the Americans did not run like sheep, and their bullets are not soft as rain! You do not belong to the Great Spirit! He does not speak to you! Where are our warriors?" Tecumseh asked with disgust. "Their bones whiten on the battlefield—the battlefield where you led them, and where you left them so that you could watch in safety beyond the reach of the Americans' rifle balls. You are not the son of my father. You are not my brother. You are the spawn of the Evil One."

Tecumseh knocked Tenskwatawa's crown from his head. The circlet of iridescent feathers broke apart and fell to the ground. He grabbed his brother by the hair and forced him to his knees.

"I have vowed never to lift my hand against another Indian, but as you have been the death of my warriors and the ruin of all I have worked for, so I shall be the death of you."

Tecumseh pulled the tomahawk from his belt and lifted the weapon high over his head.

Billy watched in horror, wondering if the Shawnee chief would really kill his only living brother. Tecumseh hesitated. An unseen hand seemed to restrain his arm.

He released his grip, and Tenskwatawa collapsed in a cringing heap at his feet.

"You are a scoundrel and a coward. You preach abstinence to others, but you drink yourself silly when you think no one will see you. But if I kill you, which is what you deserve, it will destroy any chance I have of forging this confederation. The Creek and the Seminole and the Cherokee and all the tribes I have worked so hard to unite will say I am unable to unify my own family. They will say the Shawnee nation is torn by internal strife, and they will not come when they are needed."

Tecumseh's breathing slowed to a steady pace. The flashing light in his eyes died back. The strong jaw, which had jutted forward angrily, was now lowered thoughtfully. He returned his tomahawk to his belt.

"My eyes are cleared now," he said. Nodding toward his brother, he added, "You will never again be allowed to speak with authority. You have destroyed all the work I set out to accomplish."

Tecumseh threw a handful of dirt at the man he had once called brother and banished him to the edge of the camp.

That night the Shawnee leader fell into a despondent mood. The momentary joy he had expressed on seeing Star Watcher and Cat Pouncing among the survivors dissipated when he recalled the enormity of all that had gone wrong. Billy had seen it happen on other occasions as well, when the burden of leadership became too heavy even for Tecumseh. He spoke of his people who had been scattered as if blown by the wind. He spoke of the tribes who had rejected his entreaties. He worried that he could not forge the single nation of which he dreamed.

"Their ears were deaf to me. I could not induce them to come where the water turns to stone and the rain comes from the clouds in showers of white wool and buries everything in sight."

He spoke, too, of the homeward journey. "I had to shut my eyes all the way so as not to see the beautiful country that would soon be trampled under the feet of the hated white men. I was going from a sunny clime to one of ice and snow, and I thought that, although they might lie deep and cold upon the roof of my *wegiweh*, I should find a warm fire within. And that thought kept me warm through all the chilly nights of the long journey. If I was hungry, I said, I can bear it, for my people on the Wabash have plenty of corn."

Billy stared at the flames of the small fire they had built. Even wood was scarce in this forlorn little camp. The bustling town of Tippecanoe, so filled with hope such a short time ago, had been laid waste and was empty save for the ghosts of the dead. The great army assembling there was now thrown to the wind.

Like Grandmother Kokomthena's net, Tecumseh's grand plan was unraveling.

11 · A SPY AMONG THE LONG KNIVES

Dear Father,

So you have heard of the Battle of Tippecanoe. It was good of you to send a scout here to inquire after me. I am somewhat ashamed to inform you that I am safe. I was with Tecumseh in the south when the fighting occurred.

The destruction of what many call Prophet's Town has ignited a fire among the Indians living along the Wabash River. Their hatred has flared from sparks that had been smoldering for years. It comes from watching one's children starve to death, I suppose. Small bands of warriors have painted their faces and followed the warpath. They have burned isolated cabins of American settlers and killed farmers in their fields. Tecumseh says this will fail. He knows the Americans will go to Harrison and beg him to wipe us out once and for all. We are not yet ready.

It is very disheartening.

I'll close for now, as the scout seems eager to be on his way back to Fort Malden.

*I think of you every day and pray for your continued
health.*

> *Your loving son,*
> *Billy*

Springtime had come to the Indiana Territory, and the red-
bud trees covered the wooded hills in shades of magenta. Here
and there the vibrant color was broken by splashes of white
from the blossoms of dogwood. Billy walked with Tecumseh
along Tippecanoe River. They'd been speaking of recent events
when their conversation was interrupted by the drumming of a
woodpecker in the distance. Falling silent for a moment, they
listened as the hollow tattoo echoed throughout the forest.

Billy sighed. "How pleased Harrison must be," he said, "sitting in his mansion at Grouseland with its fancy furniture and
polished floors." He'd felt angry and frustrated since they'd returned from their journey. "What should be done now? What
can *I* do?"

Tecumseh stopped walking and peered into Billy's eyes.
"Sauganash, you have been loyal when others have left. It has
been a gift of the Great Spirit that our paths have crossed.
There is much you can do . . ."

Tecumseh made Billy his courier, and Billy rode hard carrying the messages entrusted to him. He wrote letters to the
British at Fort Malden expressing Tecumseh's thanks for past
assistance and entreating the Redcoats to come to their aid
again. He acted as interpreter no matter what hour of the day
or night.

Tecumseh forced aside his personal anguish over Tippecanoe and hurried from village to village urging the warriors to

lower their tomahawks until such time as he could gather a great army. To all who would listen, he said, "I stood upon the ashes of my own home, where my own *wegiweh* sent up its fire to the Great Spirit, and there I summoned the spirits of the braves who had fallen in their vain attempt to protect their homes from the grasping invader, and as I snuffed up the smell of their blood from the ground I swore once more eternal hatred—the hatred of the avenger."

War was in the air. The nations vying for control of the Northwest Territory spoke of little else. The Americans, encouraged by their victory at Tippecanoe, pressed their government for a full-scale military campaign. The Indian nations, furious that the Treaty of Greenville had been broken, promised renewed hostilities. The British, seeing their chance to keep the fur trade, prepared for action. Billy knew that it was only a matter of time before war broke out.

Because of his mixed blood, Billy could go places that were barred to Tecumseh's Shawnee. So, one June morning in 1812, he cast aside his deerskin hunting shirt and buttoned on a loose-fitting white linen blouse with billowing sleeves. A pair of linsey-woolsey knee breeches and buckled shoes came next. He brushed his dark hair back in a queue and pulled on the kind of floppy-brimmed hat favored by American farmers. Then he rode to Detroit, his town, which was still in enemy hands.

Jingling the few silver coins in his pocket, Billy sauntered along the streets of the growing town, pleased that shopkeepers who'd known him since his schoolboy days failed to recognize him. Down at the wharves, he sat lazily on a dock piling, aimlessly whittling a piece of wood under the summer sun but in reality watching and counting as American sailors unloaded ships stockpiled with goods sent to provision the fort. Crate after crate of cannonballs and kegs by the score filled with gunpowder were gingerly carried down the gangplanks of the newly arrived schooners. Blue-coated soldiers carried boxes of rifles from the ship to the fort.

Billy watched furtively throughout the morning. *There are enough arms and ammunition to withstand a long siege*, he thought with concern. He wondered if it would ever be possible for the British and the Indians to retake the city.

From the wharf, he went to the newspaper office, slipping inside amid the hustle and bustle of reporters and typesetters. Newsboys rushed past him on their way to grab their stacks of papers. Strangers hurried in and out all day long, and Billy's presence was barely noted. The clanking of the printing press nearly deafened him. Everyone shouted to make himself heard above the din. The editor and a reporter stood at a desk reviewing an article ready to go to press.

The editor tapped the paper before him. "HULL WAS A BRAVE OFFICER IN THE WAR FOR INDEPENDENCE," he shouted.

But the reporter, a younger man, scoffed. "PERHAPS SO, BUT HE IS AN OLD MAN NOW. HE'S GROWN TOO CAUTIOUS, THEY SAY."

"A GENERAL SHOULD BE CAUTIOUS," the editor said, defending William Hull, the American governor of the Michigan Territory.

Billy guessed that he'd been made a general in anticipation of the coming war.

"NO, TRULY I SAY TO YOU," the reporter insisted, "HE HAS LOST HIS METTLE. I FEAR HE WILL MAKE A POOR COMMANDER."

Billy, who had knelt nearby as if to wipe the mud from his shoes, straightened and left.

Later, he strolled into the most popular tavern in town. It, too, was noisy, with a man singing a soldier's ballad over the shouts of the customers to the bartender. Imitating the nasal twang of the northwest farmers, Billy asked to join a game of brag with three other cardplayers seated at a table. As they slapped their aces and kings and queens on the table, they spoke of the call to arms that had been issued. The territorial militias and the regular army were swelling with new recruits.

"Who's leading the army?" Billy asked innocently.

"You *are* a country bumpkin, aren't you," the player to his right said with a laugh and a wink to his friends. He spit a wad of chewing tobacco on the floor.

"Hull will command Fort Detroit, of course. But it's Harrison the Indians and Redcoats had better look out for. Rumor has it he'll be leading a contingent of Kentuckians. And I hate to say it, being a Michigan man myself, but those Kentuckians are the best sharpshooters I ever did see."

"And they can outride anybody," his companion added.

"No sir, almost makes you feel sorry for those poor Shawnee under Tecumseh. A sergeant at the fort told me they're planning some kind of three-pronged attack against the British forts."

Another man, who had been silent until now, said, "I'd like to get my hands on that Tecumseh. Those Shawnee are nothing but trouble."

They all looked at Billy then, as if wondering why he'd said nothing.

One man squinted at him suspiciously. "What have you got to say for yourself, fella?"

Billy just couldn't bring himself to say anything ill of Tecumseh or the British. The entire tavern seemed to fall suddenly silent, and Billy felt as if everyone there was eyeing him. He knew that if they suspected him of spying they wouldn't hesitate to hang him.

"What's it gonna be," Billy asked, grinning stupidly and rubbing his hands together, "politics or cards? I need to win my money back!"

They laughed at his backwoods manner, and the conversation turned to farmers' talk and the weather. An hour later, still playing the fool, Billy apologized that he was broke and excused himself.

Racing to Tecumseh at Fort Malden, he burst into the military headquarters he'd been directed to by a sentry. There, in a room barely awash in the last light of the day, Lieutenant Colonel Thomas Bligh St. George, the commander of the fort, was surrounded by his officers, including Billy's father, who welcomed his son with a hug. Tecumseh was attended by Shabonee and the warlike Potawatomi chief Withered Hand. It had been he who had first invited Tecumseh to build a village at Tippecanoe, and they had been fast friends since that time. Matthew Elliott stood between the two groups of men, ready to be of service. It was a gathering that would be repeated many times in the months to come. As Billy entered, Lieutenant Colonel St. George was saying, "War has not been declared. My superiors have told me to do nothing until that time."

"All this blasted waiting," Billy's father complained. "We could be marshaling our men instead of sitting here doing nothing."

"There is much that can be done," Tecumseh countered. "I

can gather the Indians. The tribes in the south have counted their sticks. They know it is time to walk the red road of war."

The commander seemed surprised by Tecumseh's farsightedness.

Matthew Elliott said, "Remember the Americans can do nothing against us yet. They wait for word just as we do."

Along the frontier, news traveled only as quickly as a man on horseback. It could take weeks to receive vital information from the east. During that time, the British and the Americans watched each other warily across the wide Detroit River. They fretted and paced, all wondering anxiously what their leaders in Washington and London were deciding.

"Do you bring news, Sauganash?" Tecumseh asked.

"I do. The Americans expect to hear a declaration of war very soon. They are recruiting for their militias and the regular army. This very day schooners unloaded provisions for Fort Detroit. They are well supplied now with food and arms."

"A plague upon them!" Matthew Elliott stormed. "If we'd only acted sooner, we could have prevented it."

"It's a well-provisioned army but poorly led," Billy added, with satisfaction. "There are grave doubts about General Hull's courage. It seems his men have little confidence in him. They wonder if he has the heart for a fight."

"A frightened general . . ." Captain Calder mused, thoughtfully stroking his chin.

"We must increase his fears," Tecumseh said.

Shabonee and Withered Hand grinned. They had fought under Tecumseh before when cunning had been his main weapon. Billy wondered what the Shawnee might have in mind.

"Captain Calder," Lieutenant Colonel St. George said, "draw up a report with this information and have it sent to General Brock. He is at Fort Niagara."

With Billy's assistance, that was quickly done. Soon a mounted messenger and his escort of a few men were on their way. As they left, they passed a courier racing to Fort Malden on a lathered horse. The exhausted man was ushered into the headquarters, where he relinquished the papers he carried. The commander scanned them while the other men in the room watched the expression on his face change. Finally he looked up.

"Gentlemen," he said quietly, "war has been declared."

Matthew Elliott clasped his hands together gleefully. "Aye, that's more like it! Now we can do something."

"Sir, if I may suggest," Captain Calder said tentatively, "the Americans are provisioning themselves by ship. Would it not behoove us to send our navy to intercept any incoming American vessels? Who knows what we might find."

It was decided immediately, and orders were issued. These were fighting men, all of them, trained for warfare. They had been pacing like caged animals for months. Now they were set free, and they wasted no time. The tiny British navy set sail downriver before dawn. Tecumseh and his men returned to their nearby village and called a council to share what they had learned. Tecumseh sent riders in the four directions to spread the word and to urge the warriors to hurry. During the days that followed, Billy rarely left his side. Together, they scouted the movements of the American troops. One afternoon, concealed in the woods, they watched for hours as column after column of Ohio and Kentucky militiamen marched toward the gates of Fort Detroit. One after another, the heavy gun carriages and supply wagons rumbled past them on the road.

"They are well fed and well armed," Tecumseh said, after the last horseman of the American rear guard had passed by and the birdcalls of the forest could be heard again.

"But they are poorly led," Billy reminded him. "When can we fight?"

"A war chief does not put his men in unnecessary danger," Tecumseh cautioned. "Let us first see if we can achieve our aims with cunning."

That night Tecumseh sent his own warriors to guard the road between Detroit and the Maumee River. No more Americans must be allowed to enter Detroit. They must isolate Hull and his men like flies in a bottle.

Not long after, at another meeting in the headquarters at Fort Malden, the captain of a British ship reported with great delight that in the first move of the war they had put the Americans in check. They had spotted General Hull's hired schooner, the *Cuyahoga*, and handily seized her as she sailed north toward Detroit. The documents she carried were priceless.

The commander leafed through the dispatches, a grin slowly spreading across his face.

"Chief," he said, looking up at Tecumseh, "our opponent Hull, who as you know has been mustering troops in Ohio, has been duped. We now know exactly where the American army is at present, its size and strength, its commanders, and"—here the commander paused to savor their good fortune—"its complete battle plans."

A closer reading sobered all present when they saw that the

instructions Hull had been given were to take Fort Malden as soon as possible. Even though Tecumseh had made certain no more men and supplies would reach Detroit, the Americans already had enough soldiers and arms to cross the river and take the British fort. They must improve their defenses immediately. During the long hot weeks of July, they kept watch. Twice the Americans crossed upriver and marched almost within sight of Fort Malden. Then, inexplicably, they retreated. For many in the British fort, it remained a mystery why Hull did not crush them. He had the men and cannon to do so.

One summer night, they held an important meeting. Matthew Elliott and the other British officers joined Tecumseh and his war chiefs to plan their own attack against the Americans. Although it was well past sundown, the room was still oppressively hot. They hadn't felt a breeze for days, and the air was stale with their own sweat. Outside, languid fireflies lit the parade ground. Asked to attend as a translator, Billy unrolled the map and anchored it with candlesticks as the men gathered around the table. While moths circled the candle flames, they studied the strongholds of the Northwest Territory and Canada. Using his knife as a pointer, Billy indicated the targets the Americans had chosen to attack.

"Montreal, Niagara . . . and here, the Detroit frontier," he said.

"We must devise a plan to defeat them," Lieutenant Colonel St. George said simply.

Throughout the evening, various strategies were put forward, discussed, and seriously considered or quickly dismissed.

At midnight, Tecumseh leaned over the map and lightly

traced the rivers and lakes. He pointed out the portage trails that had been used by the Indians for generations. His eyes darted here and there across the paper as if he were studying a giant chessboard.

"We must begin in the north and the west and sweep them back whence they came," he said. He indicated Mackinac in the north. This was the gateway to the northernmost trade routes. Then the point of his knife fell upon Chicago, the growing hub for travelers to the Mississippi and the upper Great Lakes. "And here," Tecumseh concluded, thrusting his own knife through the map and into the table, where it quivered, "we must retake Detroit."

After an hour of excited discussion in the stifling room, they all agreed that this was the best course to follow.

At dawn, Indian riders set out for the far north, where Fort Mackinac guarded the water passage between the upper lakes. They carried instructions to those chiefs who had heard Tecumseh's message.

"And after Mackinac," Matthew Elliott said, "Chicago and Detroit."

A fortnight later, Tecumseh's messengers returned exultant. Mackinac was again in Indian hands! The Americans, seeing the size of the Indian force there, surrendered without firing a shot. Those victorious warriors—Ojibwa, Menominee, Sauk, Fox, and others, were now riding their painted war ponies south to join Tecumseh for his attack on Detroit.

The next day, Tecumseh repulsed a contingent of American soldiers sent by Hull to open the road to Ohio. Again they captured a mailbag with valuable information. From the dispatches enclosed, they learned that General Hull, hiding behind the walls of Fort Detroit, had become hysterical with fear of the Indians when he'd learned of Mackinac's fate. He wrote to his superiors that the fall of the fort at Mackinac *"opened the northern hive of Indians, and they were swarming down in every direction."*

Dozens of letters from the troops to their wives and families complained bitterly of Hull's cowardice and indecision.

"He drools in his beard with fear," one soldier penned in disgust.

"Sauganash, it is as you foresaw," Tecumseh said. "He hasn't the courage for a fight."

"We can win this struggle," Billy said with certainty. "I know we can."

"Now we must tell our friends in Chicago—the Potawatomi, the Winnebago, and the Fox—that the Americans are weak. This is the time to unite and defeat them. They must strike at Fort Dearborn."

Suddenly Billy remembered his old employer . . . and his family.

Although John Kinzie was officially an American, Billy would never think of him as an enemy. He knew Kinzie to be an honest man who went out of his way to help the Indians. Billy knew, too, that if Fort Dearborn fell, the Indians, in the heat of battle, might burn and loot the surrounding trading posts and perhaps massacre the tiny civilian settlement along the river. And although Jane was half-Indian, she, too, was in grave danger.

When Billy presented this dilemma to the others, the British commander cautioned him.

"If you bluntly warn John Kinzie, the trader must in good

conscience inform the American commander of the fort. It will eliminate the element of surprise for the Indians and probably cause the endeavor to fail. Many warriors might needlessly die in the struggle."

"If we say nothing," Billy countered, "John Kinzie and all the members of his household run the risk of being killed by Indians from distant tribes who know nothing of him."

There must be something that could be done.

"Tecumseh, let me go to Chicago," Billy said. "Let me speak to Kinzie—"

"No," Tecumseh said abruptly. "It will endanger our plan."

"Kinzie has been a friend to the Indians," Billy pleaded. "I won't speak openly of our plans. I will simply warn him to be on guard."

Tecumseh closed his eyes and touched the *opawaka* that hung around his neck. The planes of his face, cheekbone, and jawline, the caverns of his closed eyes, all softened in his stillness.

"Shabonee, ride with Sauganash," Tecumseh finally said, as if coming out from under a spell. "Talk to the Potawatomi chiefs. Tell them our quarrel is with the American soldiers at the fort, not the traders along the river. Remind the chiefs that Mackinac fell without firing a shot. Tell them to avoid bloodshed. They are to demand the surrender of Fort Dearborn. Only if the Americans refuse are the Potawatomi and their allies to attack. Tell them to wait until midway in the Heat Moon."

"August fifteenth," Matthew Elliott said in way of explanation to the British officers.

August 15, Billy thought anxiously. *It is less than one month from today.*

"But John Kinzie . . ." Billy began. Although it was Kinzie's name he spoke, it was Jane who commanded his thoughts.

"Shawneeawkee—Silver Man—has a good heart," Tecumseh said. "The warriors of Chicago know him and will do him no harm, but it is true, he will be a stranger to the braves from afar. He and his family will be in danger. Go to him after you have spoken to the chiefs, but do not speak openly of the attack to come."

Following Tecumseh's orders, Billy and Shabonee left early the next morning. They swam their horses across the Detroit River and hastened westward. Day after day, they rode through forest and across prairie, until a week later they reached their destination of Fort Dearborn at the mouth of the Chicago River.

Riding on alone and posing as an Irish-born frontier trader, Billy stopped at the fort on the pretext of paying his respects to the local American commander.

"And how might ye be on such a fine day as this?" he asked Captain Nathan Heald as he was shown into the officer's headquarters.

Heald looked up from his paperwork, annoyed by the interruption, while Billy continued to pepper him with innocent-sounding questions.

Soon after, Heald brusquely sent him on his way, but not before Billy had memorized the interior fortifications of the stronghold and the number, size, and placement of the artillery. Joining Shabonee at their rendezvous place in the woods, Billy shared what he'd learned during the short interview he'd been granted.

"Heald has little understanding of Indian ways, and the

Americans here seem to know nothing of the fall of Mackinac and the danger they are in."

Together they visited with the Potawatomi chiefs Black Partridge and Sits Quietly in their nearby villages. These men were revered warriors who had led their tribe through many battles. They were pleased to hear of the victory at Mackinac and promised to do all they could to avoid unnecessary bloodshed. And, yes, they would wait until midway in the Heat Moon, as Tecumseh requested.

Finally, Shabonee and Billy set out for John Kinzie's trading post on the far side of the wide river. A breeze brought the scent of ham curing. Soon they could see the smokehouse along with the bakehouse, the two barns, and the workshops. As they approached, Shabonee pointed out the trader in the corral. He was breaking a colt to the saddle. Kinzie's face was weathered and sunburned, with dust settling in the creases in his forehead. His thinning chestnut hair was pulled back neatly in a queue. When he saw Billy and Shabonee, he dropped the colt's lead rope and strode to the fence.

Billy shook his hand.

"This is a welcome surprise," Kinzie said.

Billy found himself stammering, unsure of what to say.

"Your health, sir, is it good?" he asked, feeling foolish. "And the trading post . . . how is business?"

Kinzie answered all of Billy's questions affably and asked if Billy would consider returning to his employ.

"I'm needed elsewhere now. Perhaps someday I'll return to business." He changed the subject before Kinzie could ask him more. "How are Mrs. Kinzie and the children getting on?"

"They're well. Marsh fever took five people farther up the river last year, but we escaped it."

"I'm glad to hear they're all right," Billy said.

The colt whinnied just then, tossing its lead rope into the air.

"Jane . . . how is she?" Billy continued.

"As good as gold. She's away just now, though, helping with a neighbor woman's confinement."

Billy's shoulders sank with disappointment. But he knew it was for the best; he never would have been able to withhold the truth from Jane. "Will you give her my regards, sir?"

The trader promised that he would.

Then Shabonee awkwardly suggested that Kinzie take a vacation with his family.

John Kinzie laughed. "A vacation! Are you mad? I couldn't leave my trading post at this time of year."

"Mr. Kinzie," Billy said, swallowing hard, "we're old friends. Think again on what Shabonee has said. It would be a wise thing for you to take a vacation at this time."

"Billy, I've never seen you look so serious," Kinzie said.

"The days of August grow hot, sir. The marsh air along the river is stale and breeds disease. It would be good for your family's health to be away from here. Why not go north for a few weeks?" Billy said.

The contrived conversation died, and they all looked to the high-spirited colt prancing at the far end of the corral. Kinzie's brows were drawn together in a perplexed frown. He seemed to be thinking over the meaning of this odd visit. The trader was not a fool, and Billy was hoping he would say, "Yes, perhaps we'll go away for a few weeks." But instead, Kinzie said, "I will take your advice under consideration, but I cannot leave my home."

Filled with anxiety for the safety of his friends, Billy rode with Shabonee back to Tecumseh, as he had said he would. But as they galloped their horses over the wide sunlit prairie, he wondered what more he might have said.

12 · A DEADLY GAME OF RIDDLES

I'm going back," Billy said.

Shabonee and Tecumseh both looked at him as if he'd lost his mind. They had good reason to worry. Billy had never before felt so torn, and the anxiety of the past several days showed on his face. He laughed bitterly, wishing he could be rent in two: one man to stay here and join in the fight for Detroit, one man to return to Jane and the Kinzies, to do whatever he could to protect them.

He and Shabonee had found Tecumseh at his village near Fort Malden training some of the young warriors newly arrived from upper Michigan. Leaving them to their rifle practice, the Shawnee chief led Billy and Shabonee to a grove near his *wegiweh* where they could rest in the shade.

Tenskwatawa lounged nearby, fashioning a small medicine doll. He curled his lip in disdain at Billy's approach. Tecumseh sat down with his back to his brother. Not long ago, he had reluctantly allowed him into his presence again.

"Shawneeawkee is a good man," Billy said. "I must return to Chicago. I have to make it clear to him that he should leave for a time." Although he spoke of John Kinzie, it was Jane who filled his thoughts most insistently.

"Have we not done all we can?" Shabonee asked. "Black Partridge and Sits Quietly will look after them."

"That may not be enough," Billy argued. "Tecumseh, you can spare me. If I leave today, perhaps I can reach Chicago before the fifteenth day of the Heat Moon."

Earlier, Tecumseh had said how glad he was to have Billy back, that his skills as an interpreter were needed more than ever. He did not speak immediately.

It was Tenskwatawa's complaining voice that broke the silence. "It is foolish to trouble yourself over a white man," the disagreeable medicine man said.

"Not all whites are our enemies," Tecumseh said sternly over his shoulder.

"Kinzie provided blankets and guns for us when we had need of them. He sold them to us at a fair price. He has treated us with respect," Billy said.

"You are a fool, Calder," Tenskwatawa said. "Go down to the river and wash that stinking white skin. You are no Indian."

"Your eyes are full of smoke," Tecumseh said to the medicine man. "Your ears are full of roaring waters."

"Brother," Tenskwatawa said, "you see what color he is when he says he prefers to help the whites."

"Get away from us!" Tecumseh said curtly.

The man who called himself the Prophet rose and left, muttering an imprecation under his breath.

"You won't reach them in time," Shabonee said.

"There is a chance," Billy said.

"It has been decided that we will attack Detroit at the same time that Chicago is attacked," Tecumseh said.

The news hit Billy like a blow to the face. There was nothing he wanted more than to be in the fight to retake his town. He had dreamed of it since he was a boy. Tecumseh had the men he needed, and the British had pledged their guns. This was his opportunity, the moment he had been waiting for. Should he stay or go to Chicago? He closed his eyes for a moment, his thoughts in turmoil. At first he saw only roiling colors behind his eyelids as the sun flickered through the leaves, but slowly the tempestuous sea of his mind calmed. It was Jane's face that appeared to him. Her almond-shaped blue eyes and her braided and looped black hair were as clear as if she were standing before him. The sound of her voice filled his ears like birdsong. He would give up everything to ensure her safety. Billy opened his eyes. "There are others here who can translate, but there is no one else who might convince Kinzie."

"There is none here with your breadth of knowledge," Tecumseh said.

"I'll return as soon as I can. One man will not be missed."

"Two men will not be missed," Shabonee interjected. "I will go with you."

"No, you *would* be missed," Billy argued. "I don't need you to do this."

Shabonee crossed his meaty arms over his wide chest. "That is Potawatomi country. You will be safer if I am with you," he said in his rumbling voice.

What he said made sense, and Billy sighed with relief. Although he knew it was something he must do, he had not been eager to make the dangerous passage alone. Now the question that nagged at him was: *Can we reach Chicago in time?*

Similar thoughts had occurred to the others. Tecumseh weighed the odds. Could he spare them on the slim chance of saving one white family hundreds of miles away when fighting here in Detroit would break out in days?

Billy read his face. "It is a journey of seven days, but with good horses we can do it in five," he claimed. "We can be back before a fortnight passes."

Tecumseh thought the matter over before clasping the wrist of each in a show of friendship. "Brothers, your feet are on the straight path. May the Great Spirit speed you on your way, and may I see you again before the next full moon. I need you here. I fear Detroit will not fall into our hands as Mackinac did."

Billy left Kumari behind. The mare was tired from their last journey. He and Shabonee bridled fresh horses, the fastest in Tecumseh's herd, and raced as hard as they dared, following the Potawatomi Trail. One day . . . two . . . three . . . and then four. Riding each day from dawn until sunset, they stopped only to water the animals. Then, fearing their mounts would die from exhaustion, they left them at an Indian village on the St. Joseph River to rest. There they heard from the chief that fierce braves, armed with rifles and scalp knives, had passed that way, heading for Fort Dearborn. "Many follow the warpath," the chief told them.

With a growing sense of urgency, they borrowed a canoe and paddled downriver toward Lake Michigan. Then they could travel along the shore of the lake—perhaps ninety miles—to Fort Dearborn and Kinzie's post. That route might save them half a day.

But as they drove their paddles into the water, dark clouds billowed overhead. Soon they towered like blacksmiths' anvils in the sky. Trees along the riverbank, which had been alive with chattering birds all day, became silent as the summer air suddenly turned cold. A gust of wind flipped the leaves underside up, and the willows lifted their streamer-like branches. The current surged and bucked, threatening to capsize the canoe.

They struggled to reach the shore and dragged the canoe up onto the bank. They had come nearly to the mouth of the river, and in the distance they could see Lake Michigan. A streak of lightning struck the water, followed by a deafening crack of thunder. Foamy waves pounded the beach.

It would be impossible to continue their journey for now. They used their knives to cut saplings and built a lean-to shelter.

Watching the waves crash against the shore, Shabonee said, "Evil spirits lurk in these waters." Billy nodded. It was easy to believe such a thing. Billy felt certain that the Devil himself would use all his powers to prevent them from reaching Jane in time.

Shabonee settled himself and took a corn cake from his pouch. "Thunderbirds beat their wings," he said, "and their flashing eyes make sparks in the sky." He suggested a game of bones to pass the time, but Billy said his heart was not in it. He pounded the earth in frustration. He must reach Jane.

Throughout the night, lightning spread like tracery across the heavens, while thunder groaned as if the whole world were being torn asunder. Rain fell in wind-driven sheets. The swish of trees being tossed and the occasional crack of a breaking branch filled their ears. It was impossible to sleep.

The next day passed with maddening slowness. The wind blew all day, and it rained constantly. The water was still too turbulent for the canoe. "Why did we leave the horses?" Billy railed. "Should we go back for the animals and lose another day of travel, or wait for the storm to pass?"

Shabonee answered each question calmly and logically, which infuriated Billy. He tried to pass the time with stories, but Billy would have none of it. "Don't you understand?" he shouted. "I have to get to Chicago!"

Finally the storm blew over. They set out on the lake. Their progress was slow, for the water seemed thick as syrup. But they continued on. Every moment counted now. It was the fifteenth day of the Heat Moon. Billy hoped the storm had delayed the attack. If they were too late . . .

That night, Shabonee made a birch-bark torch and fastened it to the prow of the canoe. That and the stars in the sky lit their way over the water. They forced themselves to paddle although their muscles were cramped and twisted with pain.

The next day, they made good time. The canoe skimmed over the glassy surface, and the rising sun warmed their backs.

"We should reach the fort by this afternoon," Shabonee said over his shoulder.

Between each stroke of his paddle, Billy searched the horizon for the stockade walls.

An hour later, he saw a line of smoke curling into the sky. Though he felt sick to his stomach guessing what it meant, he paddled with all his strength.

No, dear God. Don't let it be what I fear most.

They drew closer, and with Shabonee's help, Billy dragged the canoe ashore.

Scrambling up the sand dunes, they found the trail leading to the fort—or what had once been the fort. Now there was only a smoldering ruin. Overturned wagons, some burned to their skeletal framework, littered the roadside. There were scattered groups of bodies where the American soldiers and civilians of the fort had been killed. Old men, women, and children were among the dead. At his feet lay a baby cruelly torn from her mother and killed, and the mother, arms outstretched in death, a few yards away.

Why do so many warriors kill the innocent? he wondered.

Billy's throat tightened until he could barely breathe. His bowels shifted with fear and loathing. He felt so sick he thought himself incapable of another step. He had wanted so much to get here, and now he only wanted to get far away. He did not even dare to think of Jane. He cursed himself for being too late.

If he were still a boy, he could sit down and weep. But he was a man now, and he knew he must act accordingly. He must find Jane and the others and bury them.

Shabonee and Billy checked each body, looking for the trader and his family. There would be Eleanor and the four children, and Kinzie with his shrewd face and thin chestnut-colored hair. He looked for their house servants and the hired men. But there was no sign of any of them. Billy counted over one hundred dead in the area surrounding the fort, but there was no trace of the ones he loved.

Where are you, Jane?

As they stood despondent in the prairie grass, a fresh breeze brought the faint sound of victory drums to their ears. They followed the steady beat to the Indian encampment a mile away. Threading their way through the crowd, Billy and Shabonee searched until they found Chief Sits Quietly. The celebrations had begun, and it was with difficulty that Billy made himself understood over the din. He was looking for the trader John Kinzie and his family. Did the chief have knowledge of him?

Sits Quietly told them that Black Partridge was protecting them.

"Thank God . . . thank God," Billy said.

But the good news was instantly overturned. Only moments ago, a late-arriving war party had stormed from the camp. Disappointed that they'd missed the fighting, they had headed for the river, threatening to kill the Kinzies and plunder the trader's goods. Black Partridge was there now, but there would be little he could do against hostile warriors from a foreign tribe.

Billy sprinted toward the trading post with Shabonee at his heels. Following the footpath downriver, they soon spied Kinzie's place on the far side of the water. At that moment, Billy recognized Black Partridge as he parleyed with a dozen warriors Billy had never seen before. Their faces were painted black. Black Partridge was trying to placate them when the biggest and the loudest of the young braves shouldered his way past the old chief. He pulled his tomahawk from his belt as he made his way to Kinzie's front porch.

Billy's heart pounded. He had to stop them. He had not come all this way to watch Kinzie being scalped. It would be impossible for him and Shabonee and one old chief to physically stop them. Billy knew that this rescue, if he could do it, would require cunning, not strength. He did not have to overpower them; he just had to prevent them from entering the house. He remembered Tecumseh's endless array of tricks. If he could present himself in an unexpected way or do something to catch them off guard, perhaps . . .

Billy cupped his hands to his mouth and in a friendly fashion hallooed to the Indians as if they were old friends.

"Who are you?" Black Partridge shouted back, squinting.

"I am a man," Billy said, as if playing a game of riddles. "Who are you?"

"I am Black Partridge." He peered across the water. "Again I ask, who are you?"

"I am Sauganash," Billy said. He was encouraged to see the war party halt, interested in this curious exchange.

It was a name Black Partridge knew. "Come across. There are men here you should meet."

Billy's pulse beat like a bird's as he watched the hostile leader snort in disgust, turn his back, and enter the house. His men filed in behind him. Black Partridge met Billy and Shabonee at the shore after they had furiously paddled a canoe across. "Our friend Shawneeawkee is in grave danger," he said quickly.

Billy sped into the house. There, in the dining room Eleanor had worked so hard to decorate in as civilized a manner as possible, the lady of the house and her husband with their children were huddled against the wall. There, too, was Jane, comforting a small child in her arms, turning the little girl's face toward her shoulder so she would not see the black-painted warriors. Three servants cowered in the corner.

Between the Kinzies and Billy were the warriors, tomahawks and knives drawn. Their leader glowered at Billy's unwelcome entrance. Billy glanced at Shabonee. His Potawatomi friend wore a grim expression, resigned to the worst. The air of tension grew with each second. It would take only the smallest spark to ignite an explosion of violence. One word or gesture, the expression upon his face, anything, might trigger a massacre.

Very slowly Billy placed his powder horn and shot pouch on the floor, then his knife and tomahawk. He leaned his rifle against the wall. He was defenseless now. Holding his hands palms up in a gesture of nonthreatening friendship, he grinned broadly.

"Well, my friends," he said to the warriors, "a good day to you. I was told there were enemies here, but I am glad to find only fellowship. Why have you blackened your faces?" he asked with deep concern. "Is it that you are mourning the companions you have lost in battle? Or is it that you are fasting? If so, ask our friend here," he said, nodding toward Kinzie, "and he will give you food to eat. Perhaps you have never met him before, and it is good that now you have at last. Shawneeawkee is the Indians' defender and never yet refused them what they had need of."

Shabonee added, "Friends such as that always deserve the utmost of protection from those who have benefited from such kindness. It is a custom that our chief, Tecumseh, has always observed."

The leader of the angry war party was taken aback. It would not be wise to antagonize Tecumseh's two emissaries, who had obviously come to protect this white family. He turned to Billy, who smiled as if to say there was a way out of the situation that would be satisfactory to all.

The young war chief glared from behind his death mask of black paint. He seemed unwilling to give up this opportunity to return home with fresh scalps and plunder. He locked eyes with Billy and said nothing.

In the distance, the sound of the drums continued, a reminder of what had happened on the trail outside the fort. Although he smiled as if they were all old comrades or hunting companions, Billy clenched his fists tightly behind his back. If the worst happened, could he possibly reach Jane to shield her with his own body from the rain of tomahawk blows?

Billy stood rooted to the spot. He knew he mustn't move. He mustn't give any cause to alarm this dark-eyed and excitable warrior. An eternity passed.

At last the black-painted man spoke. "We have come here with our faces painted black in mourning for our friends."

He lowered his weapon, and his men followed his example.

"We have come," he said glumly, "to ask Shawneeawkee for some cloth to wrap our dead before we bury them."

Kinzie took a deep breath. He went to a back storeroom and returned carrying a full bolt of white cloth. In addition, he gave them some jerked beef, three calico shirts, a little gunpowder, knives, and some lead for making bullets. The hostile Indians took the gifts and silently left.

Billy bolted the door behind them and locked the shuttered windows. The grin that he'd worn as a mask before the war party was replaced by another expression, of love and friendship. Kinzie stood ashen-faced against the wall, Eleanor collapsed shaking into a chair, and one of the children burst into tears. Jane's lips were trembling. She had not taken her eyes from Billy's face since the moment he'd entered.

"I am sorry we were delayed in reaching you," Billy said, tucking his knife and tomahawk back into his belt. "It was Tecumseh's goal to take the fort. It was against his instructions that the civilians were massacred."

"We don't blame Tecumseh for what has happened," Kinzie said. "Yesterday Black Partridge and Sits Quietly did all they could to stem the violence." He gestured for them to be seated.

Jane handed the child she held to Eleanor. She excused herself and, looking to the servants, bade them help her prepare a meal for their rescuers.

With tender-hearted pity, Billy watched her go. If only he could have spared her this frightful scene.

"The American commander of the fort was brave but foolish," Kinzie explained. "After General Hull ordered him to abandon the fort, he promised the Indians whiskey and ammunition in exchange for a safe evacuation, but instead he destroyed the rifles and dumped the whiskey into the river before they left. The warriors became enraged and swore revenge when they learned of the deception."

Kinzie took his youngest daughter from Eleanor's trembling arms and cradled her in his lap. "The plan was for the Americans to leave the fort and march to Fort Wayne in Indiana. Mounted soldiers led the way, followed by the infantry. In the rear, the women, the sick, and the children rode in wagons. Everyone knew they were in the greatest danger. The junior officers begged Heald to disobey General Hull's orders, but the young captain refused to consider it."

Eleanor, whose hands were still shaking, took up the story. "The drummers and the pipers played 'The Dead March,'" she said, referring to the funeral song. "They knew how foolish it was to leave the safety of the fort. I think they foresaw what would happen." Her voice broke with emotion. "They played their own funeral song."

When she regained her composure, she continued, "They marched out of the fort hesitantly, reluctant to follow the orders they'd received to evacuate. We watched them from our bateau. You see, we were going to leave by boat. But John"—she nodded toward her husband—"was with the Americans."

"I'd promised the commander of the fort that I would do what I could to help lead the people safely away."

"We watched, horrified, as over a thousand Indians converged on the wagon train and began slaughtering the Americans."

"Captain Heald fought with courage, but there was little he could do. A few of us were lucky to escape," the trader said.

Everyone fell silent except for the whimpering children.

Kinzie finally said, "This morning Chief Sits Quietly promised us safe haven in his village until things calm down here."

"I want to go home to Detroit!" Eleanor cried, the strain of the past days showing on her face.

"No," Billy said quickly. "It will not be safe for you at Detroit, or Fort Wayne either. You would be wise to accept the offer of Chief Sits Quietly. You'll be safe with him."

Billy longed to be able to speak plainly to his old employer, but he could not say that Tecumseh was sending warriors against both Fort Wayne and Detroit. Kinzie looked across the table at Billy and seemed to read his mind. He did not press him for further details.

Billy excused himself and went to the kitchen. He took the liberty of dismissing the servants. "I will help your young mistress with the meal."

Though she was worn out with exhaustion and seemed thinner than he remembered, Jane had never appeared more beautiful to him. Her deep blue dress made her eyes appear as dark as blueberries. A single braid fell over her shoulder, and tendrils that had come loose curled about her face. Her skirt was already smudged with flour, the forgotten apron still hanging on its hook by the door. When she looked up, her lower lip quivered. Billy saw how hard she had tried to be strong for the others. He loved her more than ever.

"You are the pulse of my heart," Billy said, using the Irish phrase of endearment. "Your face has crowded my thoughts."

"Oh, Billy, when I saw you at the door . . ."

She stood at the table peeling potatoes with shaking hands while the pot of water boiled on the stove behind her. The knife she held clattered to the floor. Billy stepped forward and pulled her close in his arms. He gently smoothed her hair. "I have to go away again for a while, but I'll come back. Say that you'll wait for me." She pressed her head against his chest and nodded. "I will win a homeland for you," he whispered in her ear. "I will give you a country of your own where you will always be safe. We have Mackinac and now Chicago. It is our land again. I'll return for you when we are victorious in Detroit and Ohio."

"Billy!" she said, pulling away from his arms, suddenly desperate with fright. "Your victory has come at too dear a price. If you continue this way, it won't be over until all our people are dead. You have won for now, but I've seen enough of these Americans in the store to know that they will never give up. They're like locusts that fly so thick the whole sky is a snowstorm. Count your fingers all day long, but they'll come faster than you can count."

Billy's face darkened. He had not expected to hear this kind of talk from her. "Do you want me to lay down my weapons and do nothing?" he asked.

"I would have you lay down your weapons and do everything," she said. "You can protect us with your wits."

When he scoffed, she added, "Didn't you do that just now?"

"Your weakness is your woman's heart."

Jane turned on him angrily. "You have more learning than the rest of us, but you are so bullheaded. I have spent this morning digging graves. My heart's as strong as any man's!"

At that moment, John Kinzie pushed open the swinging door to the kitchen. Billy shamefacedly picked up the knife from the floor and sliced the loaf of bread on the table before him while Jane put the potatoes in the pot to boil. She gathered mugs and a pitcher of ale.

That night Billy and Shabonee bedded down on benches in John Kinzie's dining room. Billy primed and loaded his rifle and laid it by his side. Although the room was hot and airless, he had kept the windows shuttered and the door bolted. Sweat trickled down his spine. He was exhausted and every muscle ached, but he could not sleep. His eyes burned and his pulse raced. He was heartsick over what had happened. How could he have been so cruel to Jane?

No one slept well. He could hear the others tossing and turning in the upstairs bedrooms throughout the night, and several times the children cried out in terror for their mother.

The next day, Billy helped bury the dead.

13 · THE BATTLE FOR DETROIT

*I*t was a good victory," Shabonee said.

He and Billy had retrieved their horses and were riding back toward Detroit to tell Tecumseh that Kinzie was safe and that Fort Dearborn had been taken and burned to the ground.

It was noon on the third day of their journey, and they had stopped to fill their water bags at a stream. Billy cupped his hands and drank deeply. He wetted the buckskin bands around his wrists that helped to ward off the intense summer heat.

Shabonee ducked his head underwater and came up shaking himself like a dog. The black fringe of his hair lay in shiny wet strands across his forehead and around his wide face. It was then that he said, "It was a good victory."

Billy, who'd been very quiet, turned on him. "It wasn't a victory. It was a massacre. There was no need for such bloodshed. You saw the women and children!"

"The Americans lied to us—again!" Shabonee said.

"Warriors don't kill women and children. That is *poji*—the wrong way."

Stung by Billy's anger, Shabonee fell silent as they remounted and followed the trail eastward. August's heat rose from the pungent earth, giving birth to a world of buzzing insects. Fragrant meadows surrounded them like seas of yellow-petaled flowers.

Billy couldn't reconcile the beauty of the countryside with the horror of warfare. He brooded over the events of the last few days. His one goal had been to help his people, and it was now in sight. Mackinac was under British and Indian control, and Chicago, too. But they'd paid a heavier price than they realized, Billy thought. He sadly recalled the savagery of some of the warriors.

Hours passed before he brought up the subject again, and again Shabonee debated with him. "It is less than what the Americans do to us," he said fiercely.

"That may be true," Billy admitted. "I know that some American traders deliberately debauch the Indians with whiskey. Their government's treaties are riddled with lies. There have been betrayals and butchery unworthy of soldiers." He knew, too, that some of the Kentucky riflemen were in the habit of skinning the bodies of fallen Indian braves and using the human leather for razor strops. Their generals had permitted it.

"There are barbarians on both sides," he said.

"*Wajinomguk*," Shabonee said, using the Potawatomi word that meant "That's how it's going to be."

"*Watiya!*" Billy shouted in response. "*Wajinomguk?*" he repeated in disbelief. "Not if I'm there!" he vowed.

"If we do not fight, we will lose our land," Shabonee said. "Do you want it on your conscience that our people starved and you did nothing to prevent it?"

Billy stared hard at the man who had become his best friend, surprised that Shabonee doubted his resolve. "I'll never stop fighting," Billy said. "But I promise you, I'll fight like a man and I'll never shed innocent blood."

Days later, as they neared Detroit, they were met by Cat Pouncing, Tecumseh's youthful son. The handsome lad waved to them and called, "I was sent to watch the trail for you." He had his father's high cheekbones and strong jaw. Bare-chested, he wore a necklace of white shells and a breechcloth.

"My father has instructed me to take you to him," he said, wheeling his horse to join them.

When he led them directly into the town, Billy and Shabonee looked at each other in surprise.

"It is ours again," the boy said, laughing. "My father said you would be surprised."

Billy was incredulous. The fort was strong, and he had seen with his own eyes that it was well provisioned. He had assumed that it would take weeks of hard fighting to win it. But Cat Pouncing was right. There was no sign of American soldiers in the streets. Instead, the main avenue was crowded with Indians of various nations and red-coated British soldiers. Victory ballads rang from the open doors of taverns.

At the fort, they left their horses with a stable hand and went directly to the headquarters. A dozen or so gouge marks scarred the parade ground where British cannonballs had hit. A few of the buildings had taken direct hits also. But overall, the fort remained in excellent condition and bore few marks of an attack. Inside, they strode through the cool dark corridors. Cat Pouncing led the way, talking excitedly over his shoulder but telling them little real news. "My father will tell you everything. What happened in Chicago? Is it ours? Did we win? Are they still fighting?"

Shabonee cuffed him playfully on the ear. "When did you become a general? We will tell your father when we see him."

They found Tecumseh in the officers' headquarters. He appeared resplendent in the scarlet coat of a British general. His long hair was adorned with two eagle feathers, and a pair of exquisitely wrought brass-handled pistols, tucked in the sash at his waist, glistened in the sunlight that streamed through an open window. There were others there. It seemed a meeting had just ended, and a stream of warriors and British officers was filing out.

When Tecumseh saw them, his face lit up with pleasure. "The Great Spirit has brought you back."

They told him all that had happened in Chicago. Tecumseh listened solemnly. "As a young warrior," he said, "I vowed never to torture captives or shed innocent blood. We must forbid it among our men."

"Shawneeawkee and all his kin are safe," Billy said, without referring to his role in their rescue.

"It was Sauganash who saved the white family," Shabonee said.

"No," Billy replied thoughtfully. He had been as stunned as anyone when the hostile warriors had left. "It was the Great Spirit." When speaking with Tecumseh, Billy felt comfortable using the Shawnee term for God. In his own mind, he felt that it referred to the same Supreme Being to whom Père Jean-Paul prayed.

"What has happened here?" Shabonee asked excitedly.

Tecumseh told them that Detroit had been won because of the leadership of a remarkable British general.

Billy knew before asking that Tecumseh's part had not been small. He knew, too, that Tecumseh was not always so impressed by British soldiers.

"The Great Father of the Redcoats sent a new commander here. Major General Isaac Brock is a friend to the Indians," Tecumseh said. "When he came to Fort Malden, he said he would take Detroit . . . and he did."

"But how?" Billy asked. "Hull had more than two thousand men, over thirty pieces of artillery, cannon in the twenty-four-pounder class, and at least a month's supply of food. The Americans could have held out a long time."

"That is what the Redcoat officers said to Brock," Tecumseh commented. He further explained that after being informed of Hull's character, Brock had said, "Well, gentlemen, let us put our heads together and see how we can make our American general even more apprehensive."

Thus began a series of war meetings that hatched some clever tricks.

Brock and Tecumseh had planted fake documents on one of their couriers, who allowed himself to be captured by the Americans. The papers in his pouch stated that thousands of Indians were waiting to descend on Detroit, far more than Tecumseh actually had under his command.

The Shawnee chief then gathered his men and told them to march along the riverbank across from the American fort. After passing by, those in front were to duck into the woods and circle back to join the warriors at the rear of the line. They continued this ruse throughout the day so that, to any observer from the walls of Fort Detroit, Tecumseh's six hundred men appeared to be thousands.

Then, in broad daylight, Brock had his cannon taken across the river and aimed them at Hull's stronghold. That night, under cover of darkness to hide his true numbers, Tecumseh and his men sailed across the river in a flotilla of canoes. Brock followed at dawn, ferrying his army to the Detroit side.

"Brock sent General Hull a copy of this letter," Tecumseh said, taking a folded document from the table and handing it to Billy.

Billy unfolded the missive and read aloud for Shabonee's sake:

"Sir—

"The force at my disposal authorizes me to require of you the surrender of Fort Detroit. It is far from my inclination to join in a war of extermination; but you must be aware that the numerous body of Indians who have attached themselves to my troops will be beyond my control the moment the contest commences. You will find me disposed to enter into such conditions as will satisfy the most scrupulous sense of honor. Lieut. Col. M'Donnell, and Major Glegg are fully authorized to conclude any arrangement that may prevent the unnecessary effusion of blood.

"I have the honor to be your most obedient servant,

"Isaac Brock, Maj. Gen."

"I don't understand these words," Shabonee said.

"This is an old trick," Billy explained. "General Brock has used fierce words to frighten the Americans. It's like your old dog that growls at everyone."

"But, Sauganash, my old dog has few teeth."

Billy chuckled. "Ah, but if the growl is convincing . . ."

"What did Hull do?" Shabonee asked, turning to Tecumseh.

"He surrendered the fort," Tecumseh told them.

"Where are the Americans?" Billy asked, wondering if the victory here had been bloodless as at Mackinac or bloody as at Chicago.

"The Americans were taken prisoner aboard British ships and sent east."

Billy could barely believe it. He slapped his knee and laughed aloud. "Saints preserve us," he said. "General Hull fell for this trick?"

"It is as you said, Sauganash," Tecumseh replied. "This man Hull did not have the heart for a fight."

Cat Pouncing, who'd been trying to speak for some time, said, "The American flag of the Seventeen Fires was lowered, and the Redcoat flag was raised in its place. At noon, Father and General Brock rode side by side, leading their men through the streets of Detroit."

Only two moons had passed since the beginning of the war, and already the British and Indians had seized the three key forts they needed to secure their position. They knew from the letters they had captured that the Americans had lost confidence in Hull, while at the same time, hundreds of Indians had rushed to Detroit to fight with Tecumseh and his British allies. Unlike Hull, Tecumseh and Isaac Brock acted decisively, inspiring trust and loyalty among their men.

"In council, Brock speaks with a straight tongue. He is a brother to me," Tecumseh said.

Billy shook his head in amazement. "I can't believe Hull gave up the fort with barely a fight."

Tecumseh explained that Hull was so cowed at the mere thought of fighting Indians that he surrendered more than the British had ever hoped for. "Not only the fort and everything in it, but also the Northwestern Army of the United States at Detroit, and the entire Michigan Territory!"

Billy had never seen Tecumseh so elated. At last success was within their grasp. And this triumph in Detroit had been achieved with cleverness, not cruelty.

Shabonee, who'd been listening eagerly to all the details of the victory, leaned forward, his chin in his hand. "Sauganash, you and I will have no war stories to tell, while these warriors boast of their exploits around the fire."

Tecumseh reassured him. "The war is not over, my friend, and we have not yet recovered all our land. But Brock has promised me his aid, and with his army and cannon, we will yet return to our birthplace."

"This Brock must be some man," Billy said.

"Yes," Tecumseh answered thoughtfully. "He is a man."

He slid the pistols from his waist and placed them on the table. Shabonee picked one up and nodded approvingly at its weight in the palm of his hand. Billy drew its mate closer. The brass-plated handle was engraved with winding tendrils.

"Splendid workmanship," Billy said. "A gift from Brock?"

Tecumseh nodded.

"When may I meet this man?" Billy asked.

"Tonight, when the sun sleeps."

That evening, Billy accompanied Tecumseh to a state dinner given by General Brock for his allies and officers. Carriages lined the street of the home of one of the wealthiest merchants in Detroit, who had offered to host the victory celebration.

Every window of the large two-story brick house was lit, and the music of violins drifted through the open casements.

A butler welcomed them, and heads turned in wonder when they entered the front hall. Tecumseh wore a scarlet beret. His black hair fell to his shoulders. Suspended from his nose were the three tiny crosses he favored, and fastened about his neck was the medal, as large as his palm, of the Great Father of the English. A blue breechcloth covered his red leggings, which were fringed with buckskin. Treading softly in moccasins decorated with dyed porcupine quills, he took a few steps into the room.

Billy spotted his father through the crowd in his crisp new colonel's uniform, his hair neatly combed and pulled back from his face. As Billy and Tecumseh approached, they heard him arguing good-naturedly with Matthew Elliott, who rocked back on his heels, his thumbs tucked in his waistcoat pockets. "Rascal!" Elliott was saying. "You barely fired a shot, and I find you promoted to colonel!"

Billy embraced his father, overjoyed to see him again. He shook Colonel Elliott's hand. Tecumseh greeted the men by grasping their wrists in a show of friendship.

As they talked, servants drew the chairs to the edge of the parlor, and the musicians struck up a lively tune for a contredanse. The British officers and the leading men of Detroit requested the hands of their ladies. They took to the dance floor with upraised arms and interlinked fingers, creating a vaulted arch of scarlet uniforms and silk gowns. Then, couple by couple, each pair ducked lightly down the human tunnel until they had all taken a turn. Billy recognized some of the junior officers as boys who'd gone through school a few years before him. The sons of officers, they had followed the paths their fathers had taken. One saw him from across the crowded room. He waved and nudged his fellows. They lifted the glasses of punch they held in a friendly salute. A moment later, they were all drawn into the dance with the girls of the town. Billy watched with pleasure, wishing Jane were here.

The music ceased when General Brock arrived, and all the guests turned toward him as he was announced. Billy first noticed how he towered over the aide-de-camp who took his peaked regimental hat. Indeed, he was taller than any man present, and the epaulets on his shoulders seemed to measure a full yard across.

Billy whispered to Tecumseh, "He's built like a buffalo."

The general's expression was open and honest, marred only by a ragged bullet scar that crossed one eye. Walking with a limp but smiling broadly, Brock came directly to Tecumseh and saluted him.

"General Brock, this man wants to know you," Tecumseh said, placing his hand on Billy's shoulder. "To the Redcoats, he is Billy Calder, son of Colonel Calder here, but among the Indians he is called Sauganash."

Colonel Calder's eyes sparkled with pride as he explained Billy's background. "His mother was the daughter of a chief; his uncles were warriors. He's had a good education here with the Jesuits."

"It's an honor to meet you, sir," Billy said, shaking Brock's extended hand.

"He speaks many tongues," Tecumseh added. "Good words flow from his mouth."

"These are gifts you have apparently used well," Brock said.

"Have you ever considered becoming an Indian agent like Colonel Elliott here?"

"He'd be a fine addition to our little group," Matthew Elliott said.

"Colonel Elliott's recommendation is enough for me. For a young man of your background and skills, it would be a position from which you could do much good."

The major general politely took his leave and asked Tecumseh to come with him. "I want you to meet some of my officers." Billy watched, impressed by the ease with which they conversed. Tecumseh was courteous and dignified, although he appeared slightly amused when the British ladies curtsied to him. The officers snapped their heels together and bowed respectfully.

Billy turned to his father. "General Brock is lavish with his praise."

Colonel Calder agreed. "He's a born leader, and his men will do anything for him. He and Tecumseh have become fast friends."

When the butler announced that dinner was served, they strolled, talking and laughing, to the dining room, where extra tables had been brought in to seat the many guests. The tables, lit by silver candelabra, shone with hand-painted porcelain bowls. From a corner, liveried musicians played chamber music.

After the guests were seated, servants carried in platters crowned with roast suckling pig and mutton, boiled potatoes and carrots. Trays of little cakes filled with candied fruits were passed the length of the table from one delighted guest to the next. Matthew Elliott, seated by Colonel Calder, helped himself until his plate was heaped with all sorts of delicacies and good food. The wine and brandy glasses were kept full, too, and Billy's father proposed a series of toasts.

"Hear! Hear!" General Brock exclaimed after each, clearly pleased. He sat at the head of the long table like the father of a large family. And indeed it seemed that way to Billy. It had been a long time since he had felt such complete goodwill. Brock made his own series of toasts, praising each officer on his staff and making special overtures to his Indian allies. Of Tecumseh he said to his guests, "A more sagacious and gallant warrior, I believe, does not exist.

"Finally," he said, "we come to those men . . . those fine men of the British Indian Department." He raised his glass to salute Matthew Elliott and the three or four others with him. "More than translators, they explain Indian customs to the British and British customs to the Indians. Without them, we could not have forged this chain of friendship that binds our two peoples together."

Billy wondered if perhaps there was a place for him in their midst. He would consider General Brock's invitation.

Tecumseh had declined the brandy that was pressed upon him, explaining that he had found it bad for him as a young man and had since resolved to drink only water, which was then brought to him for the toasts. The British officer to his right murmured approvingly, impressed by his self-discipline. "I had been told that all Indians are drunkards," he said.

"As you can see, it is not true," Tecumseh replied, without taking offense.

Aware that many among the British considered the Indians no more than savages, Billy felt proud to be seated at Tecumseh's left. It was clear from the well-intentioned questions that were put to him that the Shawnee leader had made a very favorable impression on the King's men.

"I feel much joy," Tecumseh said, when asked to speak, "that the Great Father of the English has awakened from his long sleep and sent his soldiers to the assistance of warriors who are ready to fight."

During the weeks that followed, Billy was with Tecumseh and General Brock almost daily. He soon came to the same conclusion Tecumseh had regarding the new commander of the British army. Brock *was* quite a man. Despite his limp and the occasional use of a cane, Brock often burst into a room brimming with vitality. He was always thinking, always planning, always taking action. His energy seemed endless. He was blessed with common sense, courage, and farsightedness.

"A coalition of our forces can take the Ohio country," he said with assurance one day not long after the state dinner. "With your warriors, who know the land and fight with such courage, and my soldiers and artillery, we can create an Indian homeland."

It was as if sunlight had suddenly flooded the room after a long dreary winter. These were the words Tecumseh ached to hear. With a firm commitment from the British, he could achieve his goals. The fields and woods, the rolling hills, the lakes and rocky streams, the meadows overflowing with golden and lavender wildflowers, the forests teeming with game—his people's home could be theirs again.

"Of course, it won't be easy," Brock had continued.

No, it won't be easy, Billy thought.

They had taken the first steps. Mackinac, Chicago, and Detroit had been won. Ohio must be next. They would sweep the Americans back over the mountains. Billy was certain that this man Brock, this giant among men, held the key to their final victory.

14 · A World Rimmed with Frost and Snow

*M*y friends, I must leave you for a time," Brock said.

Billy's heart sank with disappointment.

Brock had been with them throughout the days of the Heat Moon. Now it was mid-September, and as they spoke, the clamorous honking of migrating geese sounded outside their headquarters. They had been discussing plans for pushing the Americans south of the Ohio River and for creating an independent Indian Territory that would be theirs for as long as the grass grew. Tecumseh had finished drawing a map of Ohio as fine as any surveyor's and was pointing out its features to Isaac Brock when a courier delivered a letter for the general.

"This tells of an American invasion near Niagara Falls," Brock said. "I'm needed there, but I will return shortly."

"You are needed here," Tecumseh insisted.

"Chief Tecumseh," Brock explained, "if we lose control of Lake Erie, then we will lose everything. I must go and fortify the eastern end of the lake. Do not let it weigh heavily on your heart. As I've said, I will return soon."

Billy watched Tecumseh's expression change to one of dismay. During the past weeks, he had been high-spirited and cheerful, expressing a hope for the future he said he had not felt for a long time. Daily, warriors rode through the gates of the fort to join the growing Indian force. The Miami, the Sauk, the Ojibwa, more Potawatomi, Ottawa, even some Cherokee and Creek from the far south all came to renew their allegiance to Tecumseh. The key to regaining their land lay in taking the American forts scattered across the frontier. Billy knew that with a sizable Indian force and the big British cannon under the command of a strong leader like Brock they could demolish the American garrisons.

For an hour, Tecumseh tried to persuade Brock to remain, but the general explained that he had no choice.

At last the Shawnee set his jaw in resignation, forcing himself to trust Brock's judgment. He was deeply reluctant to part with his new friend.

"May the Great Spirit be with you and bring you back to us," he said.

Billy knew from his father that the fighting at Niagara had been particularly fierce. He was worried about Brock. Shaking the general's outstretched hand, he said, "God be with you, sir."

He returned with Tecumseh to the village. They readied their weapons, and waited impatiently for Brock to return.

The leaves turned scarlet and gold and began to fall, and the horses' coats grew shaggy.

"It will be a cold winter," Tecumseh predicted.

They sat outside Tecumseh's *wegiweh* surrounded by the autumn harvest. Strings of apples hung from the rafters within. Nearby, women ground the seeds of pumpkins, squash, and sunflowers into a hearty meal for breads and stews. The sounds of a returning hunting party reached them, and soon they could see the horses laden with venison. Wives and mothers would cut the meat into thin strips and dry it on racks in the sun. The meat would be used in soups throughout the winter. With the skins, the women would sew new moccasins, dresses, and hunting shirts.

Billy and Tecumseh had been knapping pieces of shiny black obsidian into arrowheads. A small pile lay on the blanket before them. Later, they would attach each to a wooden shaft, wedging the stone arrowhead in a slit and tying it securely with twine. Finally, they would fletch the shaft with turkey feathers to make it fly straight.

It was near the time of the Hunter's Moon that a squad of British regulars rode into the Indian village. Their leader, a young man with a red queue and bushy sideburns, asked for and was brought to Tecumseh. He dismounted and grimly said, "Chief, I bring you word of Major General Isaac Brock. I regret to inform you . . ." The man's voice broke with emotion. "I regret to inform you that he has fallen in battle near Niagara. He was shot through the heart while leading his troops in a valiant charge. His replacement is on his way here."

The stricken looks on the faces of the men showed they felt no one could replace Brock.

The news shattered Tecumseh. He could say nothing, and it was Billy who stepped forward and thanked the men for relaying the sad tidings.

After the Redcoats left, Tecumseh turned to the young man who had become his devoted aide. He said solemnly, "They will put him in a box and bury him in the earth, following the ways of his own people." Then he added quietly, as if to himself, "If he were Shawnee, we would paint his face so that the Great Spirit would recognize him as one of his own. We would line his grave with bark and gently lay him there with his head to the west." He paused and clenched his jaw as though trying to control his emotions. "Over his body, we would sprinkle tobacco, and an elder would pray that he would be restored to life in the other world. There, by his grave, we would light a small fire to brighten his way to the Great Spirit. And, there, too, we would weep quietly and wish him well on his journey."

Tecumseh looked to the west, toward the river and lakes, the prairie, and the great sea beyond, as if hoping for a glimpse of his friend on his way to the other world.

After a moment of thought, he asked, "He will go to your God, Sauganash?"

"Yes. He was a good man, so he will go to God. And he'll live with powerful spirits called angels," Billy said.

Tecumseh seemed satisfied with this answer. He grew very quiet and said little the rest of that day, and the day after.

Autumn drew to an end, and as the last leaves curled up and fell, so, too, Tecumseh's will to fight seemed to shrivel. He set aside his arrows and tomahawk.

"Winter is coming," he said. "The British will fight no more until spring." He retreated to a village in Indiana, telling Billy that perhaps he would see him again when buds formed on the trees.

Billy realized how awful it must be to lose a good friend. He remembered how sick with worry he had been over Jane and the Kinzies. And last summer in a fierce little firefight, Shabonee had been shot in the head. The heavy ear disk he always wore spun to the ground. Billy had sprung from his place of concealment behind a tree to assist him, and as he did so his own eagle feather was clipped from his head by a sniper's bullet. But the danger to himself meant nothing when he saw blood flowing from Shabonee's head. Stunned, Shabonee reached up and touched the wound, complaining sourly that he'd lost his earring. He'd only been grazed by the bullet, and Billy had wept tears of joy when he realized his friend would live.

They had all laughed about it that night.

Now, he thought he understood why Tecumseh wanted solitude. Billy, however, chose to remain near Detroit. It was his home, and at last it was under the control of his father's and mother's peoples.

But the Americans gave them no rest. Contrary to the custom of hunkering down in winter quarters during the cold months, they had pressed back with brutal vigor. Their defeats over the summer seemed to catapult them into action. That November, Kentuckians, the fiercest of the American fighters, rode into Indiana and burned every Indian village in their path, including the newly rebuilt Tippecanoe. They dug up the corn that had been carefully stored in underground caches, and destroyed it. Once more, Indian children sickened and died from hunger.

Then, in early December, William Henry Harrison sent a force into the country of the Miami, the parcel of land that had been given to them in the Greenville Treaty. In the uneven battles that followed, the once-proud Ohio tribe was all but wiped out.

Billy dejectedly watched the snow fall from inside his father's riverside house. A cold spell had seized the countryside, and a blizzard had raged for days. Pine boughs snapped under their heavy blankets of snow. A man's spit would crackle and freeze before it hit the ground.

Turning from the window, Billy said to his father, "I don't believe we've seen such weather in years. A man needs snow-shoes just to get from his house to his barn."

Colonel Calder, who was warming his hands around a mug of steaming tea, said, "It surely is as cold as a witch's kiss."

By the end of December, the ice on Lake Erie was over three feet thick, and even the Detroit River, which because of its swift current usually stayed open, was frozen solid, so that horse-drawn sledges could cross its surface.

After Brock's death, the British sent General Henry Proctor, a taciturn and narrow-minded officer, to take command of the British forces in Upper Canada. He directed a detachment of his own men and an Indian force to take up winter quarters at Frenchtown, a small settlement on the River Raisin just south of Detroit. It was only thirty six miles away from the Americans' stronghold on the Maumee River. At Frenchtown, they would act as a buffer should the Long Knives try to recapture Detroit in the spring. Leaving his father's snug home, Billy, who had accepted a position as captain in the British Indian Department, volunteered to act as a liaison between the British and the Indian forces.

He was warming himself before the barracks fireplace on a bitterly cold afternoon when he heard a sharp noise in the distance. A moment later, one of the sentries burst into the room.

"The Americans are attacking!" he cried in alarm.

"You're mad," Billy said. "No one would march his men through knee-deep snow."

At that moment a canister of grapeshot exploded, blowing

out two of the windows and sending icicles flying like spears. Billy threw on his coat, snatched his rifle, and dashed outside. Racing from house to house where his men were billeted, he shouted orders and rallied his troops. He translated commands from the British officers into different Indian languages. Redcoats and braves fought side by side for three hours under a heavy American bombardment. But with few artillery pieces of their own for defense, they were finally driven from the town into the surrounding woods. Under cover of darkness, they made their way back to Fort Malden, where General Proctor, outraged at the gall of the Americans, ordered a retaliatory raid.

Without stopping to rest, Billy spent the next twenty-four hours on horseback, galloping through the snow from village to village urgently calling the Indians to assemble at Fort Malden.

"Hurry!" he shouted. "Wake up! Seize your weapons!" He threw his head back and harshly shouted the war cry. "AI-AI-AI-AI!"

Everywhere he went, men poured out of their longhouses and *wegiwehs* armed and ready to take the warpath.

The next day, before dawn touched the sky, the gates of Fort Malden swung open to a world rimmed with frost and snow. Black trees rose starkly silhouetted against a powdery landscape of gray and blue. A lonely wind whistled. Billy rode at the head of the Indian force that followed Proctor's foot soldiers and cavalry as they crossed the ice-bound Detroit River. The great gun carriages rumbled over the ice pack, which reverberated with otherworldly groans as the army wound its way around mountains of shimmering ice. Slowly, a feeble sun rose in the frigid sky. Its light glinted off the polished brass fittings of the rifles. Bayonet tips glittered like diamonds.

Billy yelled the war cry, "AI-AI-AI-AI!" and others along the line repeated it. Their cries pierced the raw air.

By nightfall, they had marched through the snow to within a few miles of Frenchtown. They left a handful of men there to tend the fires. "Let the Americans think we've camped here for the night," Proctor said. He led the rest of the force through the dark woods, lit only by pale moonlight, to within a few hundred yards of the town. They positioned their six cannon and waited.

"Soon we shall wake the Americans," Billy said to the Potawatomi men under his command. He tucked his cold hands inside his sleeves.

In the pink light just before the sun rose, their cannon exploded, ripping the silence with a thunderous blast. Moments later, they could see American soldiers running helter-skelter through the streets of the town, shadowy figures darting about in panic. Many of the men were killed and scalped, and their general was quickly captured. Proctor instructed his captive to have his remaining soldiers surrender or face total destruction.

"It is to your benefit, sir," Proctor added haughtily, indicating his artillery. "As you can see for yourself, it is in our power to completely destroy this town and everyone in it."

"We will surrender," the American said, "only insofar as you will agree to give us protection from the Indians."

Billy was glad to hear Proctor reassure the officer that they would be treated honorably as prisoners of war. He could not bear the thought of another massacre like the one he had seen in Chicago. But within the hour, Proctor left for Fort Malden, leaving only one of his officers behind to protect the captured and wounded Americans.

"You must not, sir," Billy argued, holding the general's stirrup. "Their blood is up," he said, referring to the most violent of the braves. "They'll think only of past wrongs and will exact vengeance against these prisoners who are helpless."

"Then you, Captain Calder, must see to it that they do not," Proctor answered. "I understand that you are part Indian. Speak to your people and control them—if you can."

"Sir . . ." Billy pleaded, astounded by the general's negligence.

"Are you incapable of dealing with the situation, Calder? Oh, very well," he said, snorting, "I shall send Colonel Elliott to your assistance when I return to Fort Malden." He priggishly adjusted his hat, spurred his horse, and rode away from Frenchtown.

Almost as soon as he was out of earshot, several hot-blooded warriors set fire to the log barracks housing the American wounded. When Billy heard the screams of the dying, he rushed back into the town. Flames shot from the windows. Those who could walk were staggering through the door, only to be clubbed by painted braves who'd gathered on the porch. Billy pushed past them but was driven back by the intense heat within. Two Americans nearly trampled him in their panic to flee, one with his shirt on fire. Billy shouldered his way through in an effort to reach the others. Smoke stung his eyes, and the heat seared his throat. The groan of rending wood sounded above the crackle and roar of the flames. The roof collapsed before him, crushing everyone within. Billy staggered back, choking for air, his face blackened by smoke.

Disgusted, Billy turned away. He'd been unable to help the poor wretches trapped in the barracks, but there were other captives held in the town. These he must lead safely back to Fort Malden. Proctor had promised them safety, and Billy would keep that promise to those who were left. The survivors had to be taken to Fort Malden, where they could be transferred safely to prison ships. He was determined that not a single man in his charge would be harmed, but neither would any be allowed to escape to sound the alarm among the Americans in their Ohio forts.

He gathered the prisoners where they were being held in other homes throughout the town. Many were barefoot, having jumped from their beds as the firing began. Most had no coats. As they marched north, the line of cold and wounded men strung out. It was impossible for Billy to supervise the entire length. As prisoners weakened along the way, some of their captors killed and scalped them.

"*Ke'go!* Stop! It is unmanly!" Billy shouted whenever he came across men who would do such things. "*Ke'batse'*—this is wrong."

A fracas in the woods commanded his attention. He turned to see a group of his own warriors pursuing twenty-five prisoners as they tried to escape through the deep snow. Billy floundered through waist-high drifts after them. "They must not be allowed to reach Harrison!" he shouted.

The Americans were surrounded and tomahawks felled several before Billy could stop the carnage. Switching from one tribe's language to another, he angrily chastised his men. "Stop the killing! Is there no room in your hearts for pity?"

He found the ranking officer among the prisoners, a Kentuckian by his accent, Billy guessed, wearing the insignia of a major. Billy grabbed him by the arm and pulled him away from the menacing braves. In three different Indian tongues, he shouted furiously, "*Stop the killing!*"

The Kentuckian's eyes glittered with fear. He pulled a slender dirk from his coat. War whoops filled the air. A warrior shouted, "Look out, Sauganash, he's going to stab you!"

Billy saw the look on the man's face. It was all wrong. In an instant, he understood. The major had seen an Indian with a blackened face, armed with a knife and a tomahawk, shouting wildly in savage tongues. Many of his comrades had already been killed before his eyes.

Billy released the major's arm and sprang lightly away from the arc of the flashing knife. But on landing, his foot caught on a tree root. In an instant, he lay sprawled, flat on his back in the snow. The Kentuckian leaped upon him, driving his knife deep into Billy's neck. Billy gripped the blade with all his strength as his attacker tried to twist the weapon. He felt the dirk slice into the palm of his hand. His vision darkened.

Immediately, a barrage of gunfire exploded in the snowy woods as every man in Billy's party came to his aid. The American major fell, struck by numerous rifle balls.

A guttural cry erupted from the throat of a warrior, "Kill all the dogs!"

The deafening noise of war whoops and rifle fire continued for what seemed forever. It echoed throughout the forest. The ground vibrated with the noise. Then silence fell, followed by the crunch of snow as concerned braves circled Billy.

Billy heard the soothing voice of a friend as the knife was gently slid from his throat. Overhead, he saw the lavender sky laced with skeletal branches clawing the heavens. Weakness overcame him. He couldn't move. The blood seemed to have left all his limbs. Neither could he think clearly. He found himself wondering if Jane was nearby. He thought he heard her voice. He felt the warm soft buzzard down, which was used by the Shawnee to stanch the flow of blood, as it was gently packed in the puncture wound in his neck and placed in the crease of his sliced hand. They wrapped him in a thick buffalo robe while old Matthew Elliott was called to the scene.

As a wintry darkness fell, Billy was tenderly lifted into a makeshift bed on a sleigh and carried over the ice and snow to his father's house.

15 · SAINTS AND SNOW SNAKES

When Billy awoke, he didn't at first recognize his whereabouts. He lay in a comfortable bed covered by a warm quilt. Someone had dressed him in a clean nightshirt. There was a small table by the bedside and a single chair. A fire flickered in the hearth, and the pungent smell of an oil lamp filled his nostrils. Finally, his head stopped swimming long enough for him to realize that he was in his father's home in the back bedroom usually kept for guests.

He had awakened during the evening after being unconscious for a full day. He lifted his hand to his neck at the odd sensation of the blood-soaked bandage covering his throat. His hand, too, was wrapped in bandages. He remembered, then, what had happened.

Billy didn't know that Colonel Calder had pulled the curtains shut so that his terrified servants would not have to see the returning Indian war parties carrying American scalps on poles through the streets and outlying lanes of Amherstburg. His father had been unable to drown out the noise, however, and Billy had awakened to the war whoops. He alone in his father's household could interpret those songs, for the different cries signaled the number of enemy killed or captured. The death chants continued for hours. He felt overwhelmed by despair, knowing he had failed to stop the slaughter. *Could there really have been over three hundred killed?* he wondered.

His father rarely left his side during those first days. When Billy was feverish, Colonel Calder pressed a cool cloth to his forehead. When he shook with chills, his father slid a warming pan beneath the covers. He washed Billy's wounds and wrapped them in clean bandages.

Billy sank into the mattress like a wraith. His throat felt as if it had been packed with hot coals. He couldn't eat. He could barely breathe. He found himself wondering in an uninterested manner if he would live. It didn't matter, he thought. He had failed miserably. He had been unable to control the men under his command. How ironic the whole thing was, he thought. It had been his efforts to save the life of an enemy that had caused him to be attacked, and it had been his men's love for him that had triggered the massacre he had hoped to avoid.

One night, as he thrashed in the grip of a fever, Billy confessed in a whisper to his father that he longed to die. He was tired of the unending anguish he felt. Dark circles shadowed his eyes. Colonel Calder straightened the rumpled bed linens and put a wet cloth on Billy's head.

"Dying is easy," his father gently rebuked him. "You just lie down and close your eyes. It's the living that's tough, lad."

In a rasping voice choked with emotion, Billy whispered, "Father, I tried to stop the slaughter." Then he remembered the cry—*Kill all the dogs!*—and the explosion of gunfire around him. Billy found himself barely able to continue. "I wanted to save that man's life," he said. "Instead, I am the cause of his death . . . and that of many others."

"No, lad, it's not your fault," Colonel Calder said. "There was nothing more you could have done that you did not do. It is Proctor's fault. He left too few officers to keep order."

Billy turned his face to the wall unconvinced and said no more. During the days that followed, whether he was awake or asleep, the remembered shrieks of the returning war parties rang in his ears.

The time of the Ice Moon ended, and the weeks of the Hunger Moon began. Billy slept on and off, unaware if it was day or night. At times, he remembered his father coming in and gently spooning warm broth between his lips.

Now and then he heard his father's robust voice as he sang an Irish lament called "Dark Rosaleen." It was a lyrical poem, and Billy recognized the words as a sad love song for Ireland. But one night it seemed to have been written for him and Jane, about the ravishing, heartbreaking beauty of the lake country.

> *O my dark Rosaleen,*
> *Do not sigh, do not weep . . .*
> *My dark Rosaleen!*
> *My gifts to you*
> *Shall glad your heart, shall give you hope,*
> *Shall give you health, and help, and hope . . .*

Colonel Calder must have gone into another room to fetch something, for the song trailed off momentarily before returning full-throated in the rich stirring tenor of his voice.

> *Over the hills, and through the dales,*
> *Have I roamed for your sake;*

> *All yesterday I sailed with sails*
> *On river and on lake.*
> *The Erne, at its highest flood,*
> *I dashed across unseen,*
> *For there was lightning in my blood,*
> *My dark Rosaleen!*

In a feverish state of half-waking, half-sleeping, Billy drew in the words: *For there was lightning in my blood . . .* He wanted to be the kind of man who had lightning in his blood. Instead, he had proven himself a weakling, incapable of controlling men under his command.

> *All day long, in unrest,*
> *To and fro, do I move . . .*
> *Woe and pain, pain and woe,*
> *Are my lot night and noon,*
> *To see your bright face clouded so,*
> *Like to the mournful moon . . .*
> *Oh! the Erne shall run red*
> *With redundance of blood,*
> *The earth shall rock beneath our tread,*
> *And flames wrap hill and wood,*
> *And gun-peal, and slogan-cry*
> *Wake many a glen serene.*
> *Ere you shall fade, ere you shall die,*
> *My dark Rosaleen!*

Billy drifted off into a disturbed sleep before the song ended.

Later that night, Billy heard his father's booted footsteps in the hallway. Colonel Calder opened the bedroom door so that a sliver of golden light fell into the room.

Billy raised his head with difficulty. "Father, can you sit with me a spell?" His voice was still hoarse from the wound.

His father stoked the fire in the hearth until the flames jumped. He sat by Billy's side as he had each day since his son had been carried home. "How are you feeling?" he asked.

"A little better," Billy said, slowly closing his hand into a fist to show that the wound across his palm was healing.

"The servants tell me you ate a wee bit more today. That's good. You've grown too thin. By the way, one of your men brought your satchel," he said, pointing to the traveling bag that had been brought in while Billy lay ill.

After his father left, Billy emptied the bag. A pouch of bullets fell out, and a small tinderbox, followed by a parcel wrapped in oilcloth. It was the book Père Jean-Paul had given him long ago. Billy paged through it, stopping now and then to read. He knew it had been written by a soldier, a man who had been wounded in battle. Billy read one passage slowly. The soldier had written: *See what the people on earth are doing—wounding and killing* . . . Yes, this man understood, Billy thought.

Farther along, tucked within the pages of the book, was the letter Jane had written him long ago. Its folds were sharply creased, and it was smudged with dirt from the many times he had read it alone in the quiet of some out-of-the-way woods. He tenderly caressed the paper, but he couldn't bring himself to look at her handwriting. He was certain that she would be sorely disappointed in him.

Billy replaced the letter and closed the book. He hadn't the strength to read any more.

He tried to speak of these things to his father. "If only Tecumseh had been there," Billy said, returning to the topic that consumed him with guilt.

"When he heard of the battle, Tecumseh sent runners here to inquire after you. I told them to say you would not return to this campaign."

"No, Father. I must return."

Colonel Calder shook his head. "There is more than one way to skin a cat," he said, tucking the blanket around his son. "You can help the Indians in other ways."

When Billy began to protest, his father shushed him and said, "Rest now."

The next morning, his father opened the curtains where the window looked out upon a snow-covered field. Billy took his first steps since the massacre on the River Raisin. Moving from the bed to the chair by the window, he wrapped himself in blankets and watched as boys from the nearby Indian camp played a game of snow snake.

They raced across the meadow in their thick moose-hide moccasins, hugging brightly colored blankets around them. Having played the game himself as a lad, Billy recognized the sticks they carried. The snow snakes were limbs of maple wood five or six feet long. The thicker end was carved to resemble a snake's head. Alternating bands of bark were peeled away before the shaft was smoked over a fire. Then the remaining bark was removed. The result was a staff with beautiful patterns of stripes or spirals.

Laughter erupted as they grabbed one small boy and dragged

him, shrieking with glee, to create an alley of packed snow. Then the game began. The biggest boy thrust his snow snake down the alley. It slid, almost sizzling, across the icy surface. He ran to where it stopped and stood it upright in the snow, daring his friends to do better. The next player heaved his snake, and it passed the first. He boasted triumphantly. Each lad took a turn until finally the winner claimed all the snakes.

The boys spent an hour this way. First a tall boy in a trapper's blanket won. Then they played a second round, and a squat, barrel-chested boy collected all the poles. The air rang with their cheering, their breath coming in puffs of frosty air sweeping around their fur caps. When they left, Billy returned to his bed, tired from simply watching the vigorous game. Their innocent competition seemed too brief a respite from the war.

Day followed day, and week followed week as Billy gradually grew stronger. His appetite returned, and his clothes no longer hung from his shoulders like a scarecrow's. The wounds on his palm and throat healed to ragged pink scars. The nightmares, which had left him sweating amid twisted bedclothes, came less often. Outside his father's house, the snow melted away, and wagon wheels churned ruts of mud in the lane.

At Billy's request, Colonel Calder often played his fiddle while his son tapped his fingers to the music. He learned the words to "Green Grow the Rushes, O" and sang it with his father along with other ballads he'd known since his childhood. When his father grew tired of playing, they spoke of small domestic matters, of families venturing out to tap for maple syrup, or the number of spring lambs born to a neighbor's flock.

One afternoon during the Wet Moon, there came a knock at the door, and Colonel Calder welcomed a visitor. Moments later, a well-proportioned athletic figure filled Billy's bedroom door. He wore a turban wound about his head with a handsome fur tail swinging from its folds.

"Tecumseh!" Billy cried, setting aside the book he'd been reading. He pulled himself up in bed.

The Shawnee chief strode into the room and stood his rifle in a corner. He nodded in greeting and sat in the offered chair for some time before speaking. The lines that had creased his face after Brock's death were gone.

"Your father says you are better," he finally said.

"Yes, I am much improved."

"You were fighting while I was sitting in a warm *wegiweh*," Tecumseh said, blaming himself. "But the story of your courage has roused me from my sleep. I have ridden as far west as the great Mississippi and north to Wisconsin and south to the Sangamon River to tell the tribes that now is the time. Shabonee and his braves among the Potawatomi are on their way here, as are the Huron, the Creek, and the Cherokee. Although the great chief Brock walks with the angels now and Proctor is but a shadow of a man, I have decided that we must go on. We must fight . . ."

When Billy tried to explain what had happened at the little town on the River Raisin, Tecumseh said, "We will fight like men. Warriors do not torture their prisoners. That is the work of cowards." Then he turned the subject. "The Redcoats have promised me that they will be our friends in this fight. This year we will take back Ohio."

Billy was encouraged, but he doubted their manpower

would be sufficient. He knew the warriors had drifted away after the fighting at Frenchtown. If they could gather several hundred men, they might have a chance.

"How many men have answered your war call?"

Light glinted in Tecumseh's eyes, and a grin began at the corners of his mouth. He lifted his chin proudly. "There are three thousand warriors here."

Billy's mouth fell open in disbelief.

It was the largest Indian force ever assembled.

16 · Go and Put On Petticoats

"We cannot trust him," Billy said to Tecumseh after they left their first meeting with General Henry Proctor.

A gloomy April rain fell as they walked back to the Indian village near Fort Malden.

The general had a reputation for disliking Indians, and the conference had borne out their worst suspicions. He had treated Tecumseh with contempt, steadfastly refusing to consider advice from the chief or confide battle plans to him. No, the meeting had not gone well. The tense scene replayed itself in Billy's mind as they continued on in silence.

Surrounded by Fort Malden's top officers, Proctor had spoken to Tecumseh as one would to an errant child.

"Chief," he had said, "the massacre at Frenchtown on the River Raisin last January has united and inflamed the Americans to a degree that they did not before feel. Harrison has soldiers rushing to join his army in unprecedented numbers."

"I was not at the River Raisin, as you know," Tecumseh said calmly. "Had I been there, I would have forbidden the torture.

I am aware that you promised the captured Americans protection but failed to provide it."

Proctor reddened. He had not expected to be called to account by a savage.

Billy's thoughts wandered. He knew that Proctor mockingly called Tecumseh "the King of the Woods" to his men. The man was woefully ignorant of Indian ways and showed no inclination to learn them. He could not possibly be more unlike Isaac Brock, who had generously extended his hand in friendship and respect.

"We have other matters to which we must direct our attention," Proctor finally said, disdainfully. He opened a map from the papers he'd held and spread it on the table before them. "General Harrison is at this very moment building Fort Meigs on the Maumee River."

"I know that country well," Tecumseh said. "He is building it near the place we call Fallen Timbers. He wants to remind us of our past defeat." Tecumseh pointed to the map at the exact spot of the new fort.

Proctor, who knew nothing of the Ohio countryside, did not bother to look.

"We must strike before the fort is completed," Tecumseh added. "We must not allow the Americans to burrow in there."

"I shall give orders," General Proctor said curtly. His officers, who'd grown to admire Tecumseh when he served with Brock, shifted uncomfortably as Proctor continued. "We'll be soon joined by the British fleet under young Lieutenant Barclay's command."

The general pointed to the map showing the harbors and shipbuilding yards along the south shore of Lake Erie. "The Americans have recently built their own fleet. Now they threaten us on the water. It is essential that we keep our supply lines on the lake open. If we can do that, we will be successful."

Tecumseh always fought on land, and his men were accustomed to foraging for themselves while they were on the warpath. He was not interested in securing British supply lines on the lake. He did, however, thoroughly understand the importance of attacking Fort Meigs before it was completed. "We must first take this fort, then your young Barclay can fight on the lake."

Tecumseh then spoke of the matter uppermost in his thoughts. "And when that is done, General Proctor," he said, holding the Englishman motionless with the intensity of his gaze, "I will need your assurance that our Great Father across the sea will return our homeland to us."

When Proctor wavered, he quickly added, "This is what our good friend Isaac Brock promised."

Proctor compressed his lips in anger and breathed heavily through his nose.

The general chose his words carefully. "I cannot speak for the King, but I will assure you that the Indians will be compensated with land. And," he added, thinking this might please Tecumseh even more, "should we capture General Harrison, he is your prisoner to do with as you wish."

Tecumseh was disgusted by the implication that his goal was to torture Harrison. He folded his arms across his chest and spoke no more. His gaze fell upon the scene beyond the window as if he had heard all he cared to hear. Proctor, meanwhile, spoke at length of other military matters as his junior officers fidgeted. Billy and Tecumseh left shortly afterward.

Now, as the thatch-roofed *wegiwehs* of the Indian village

came into view, Tecumseh said, "Summon Shabonee and the other chiefs. We will take our men and go to this fort while these Englishmen sit here and wait."

No, Billy thought, as he and Tecumseh made their way through the mud, *it had not gone well.*

Before the end of the Wet Moon, Tecumseh had assembled his combined Indian force on the ridges surrounding Harrison's new fort. Below them, the wide Maumee River flowed gently to Lake Erie.

He lifted a spyglass to his eye and studied the structure. His war chiefs gathered around him waiting to hear his assessment. Tecumseh spoke in short bursts so Billy could translate his observations into different tongues. "The fort is surrounded by a ditch . . . There are three large blockhouses and four smaller gun posts . . . The Long Knives have dug trenches throughout the parade ground where they will be safe from our arrows . . ."

Tecumseh angrily collapsed the spyglass and tucked it in his sash. "We can do nothing until the Redcoats come with their cannon."

Billy completed the final translation and listened dejectedly to the grumbling among the chiefs. As they argued among themselves about the lost opportunity, a Shawnee scout found them. The news he carried was not good. Reinforcements were riding to Harrison's aid. They would arrive within several days.

"We must fight before Harrison's army is complete," Tecumseh said.

That night, Tecumseh presented a bold plan to all his war chiefs. At first they tried to dissuade him, saying it was far too dangerous, that Harrison could never be trusted. Had he not proved himself a liar time after time? And besides, did they not have the largest army they had ever assembled? This plan would not be fair to the young warriors who had come to prove themselves in battle.

But Tecumseh would not hear their arguments. As he had many times before when faced with a united opposition, he persuaded them to see the wisdom of his decision. "Listen to what I say," he began.

Slowly, as the evening wore on, they agreed one by one to obey his wishes. But Billy saw that not one of them was at ease with this plan. And for the first time in nearly three years, Billy vehemently opposed his war chief's counsel. Reluctantly, he wrote the message Tecumseh dictated to him:

To Governor Harrison,

We are enemies and we are met here to oppose one another at last. Why should not we, who are the leaders, settle the matter between us alone, so that the blood of our fine young men need not be shed in the fight which presents itself? Meet me in combat on a neutral ground of your choice and with whatever weapon is your choice, or even with none, and I will have the same, or none, and we will then fight this matter out between us until one of us is dead. He who triumphs will then hold this ground and he who has been beaten, his people will immediately return home and remain quiet ever after. My chiefs are in agreement on this head. We are men. Let us meet like men. Let us fight like men. Let us spare our people. I await your answer. Swing a lantern above the gate if you accept. I will be watching and I will then come and meet you for the contest.

Tecumseh took the quill pen from Billy's fingers and signed his name below the message. He wrapped the paper around the shaft of an arrow and shot it over the walls of the fort.

"What will happen if he should agree to it?" Billy argued. "What if you're killed in single combat with him? There is no one who can take your place."

"If I am killed, you must lead our people to a new home."

Billy laughed in a sort of desperation. "I could never—"

"You," Tecumseh repeated, "your father, Matthew Elliott, Shabonee, Withered Hand, and the other chiefs. You must all protect the Indians. They are in great danger.

"Sauganash," Tecumseh continued, looking out over the Indian encampment, "you love our people as I do. They know you. They trust you. You speak with a straight tongue. You can explain the ways of the white man to them. If the Great Spirit calls me in battle, you will be here to help our people."

Billy shook his head. His goal had been to serve the Indians as a warrior, and this he had done. When Tecumseh had urged him to accept a captaincy in the British Indian Department, he had gladly agreed. He had been useful as a liaison between the peoples, translating, writing letters, and explaining customs. But for the Shawnee chieftain to suggest that Billy should take on a greater role if he died was preposterous. Billy could never do it.

When three hours passed and they failed to see a lantern, Billy was more relieved than anyone.

Not long afterward, Proctor arrived with his soldiers and cannon. The British general positioned his artillery on the ridges above the fort and ordered the bombardment of Fort Meigs.

Thunderous shelling continued day and night for three full days. When the smoke cleared, Proctor sent a junior officer to the Americans demanding their surrender. The man returned with Harrison's refusal. Billy wasn't surprised. He could not imagine Harrison surrendering the fort under any conditions. He was proud and would never agree to having such a blot on his record.

Later that week, by the light of a campfire, Billy wrote a letter. By his side, Shabonee sat playing with a set of painted sticks, waiting patiently for Billy to finish so they could begin the guessing game they had planned.

Shabonee looked over Billy's shoulder. "You are writing another letter to your father?" he asked.

"No, this is for my teacher, the black robe at the mission school in Detroit I told you of."

"Tell the black robe that Shabonee of the Potawatomi tribe is well. Tell him that Shabonee is the most feared warrior between the land of the Mohawk and the country of the Ojibwa. Say that his feet are as swift as forked lightning, his arm like the thunderbolt. Tell him that the Americans tremble with fear at the mention of Shabonee's name."

Billy laughed. "I'm almost finished," he said. "Then the great Shabonee can match wits with the legendary Sauganash in a game of sticks!"

Billy reread the note quickly.

Dear Père Jean-Paul,

You ask me how I am and how I spend my days.

I am well, fully recovered from my injuries, although I feel the old wounds sometimes when there is a rainfall. As for how I spend my days—a soldier's life is not as I expected it to be. There are long hours of waiting during which time we clean our rifles . . . over and over again.

Harrison has burrowed down like a fox in his den and nothing we do can induce him to come out and fight. When Tecumseh's invitation to single combat failed to elicit a response, he devised a plan that would have impressed Caesar himself. He had some of us who speak English dress in captured American uniforms. We staged a mock battle near the walls of the fort as if we were Harrison's expected troops being attacked by the Indians. Those of us playing Americans shouted for help from our "comrades" within the fort. Some of us fell from our mounts feigning death. Others cried out as if mortally wounded. We begged for aid.

It discommodes me more than I can possibly say that Harrison did not fall for the trick. The gates remained barred. These Americans are more clever and tenacious than I had thought.

I wish I knew what the future held.

As to your final question: yes, good teacher, I begin and end each day with a prayer, and among my prayers today was the hope that I might see you again soon.

May God grant you good health.

Billy

Billy tucked the note in his pocket. He would send it in the morning with other dispatches for Detroit. Then he gave his full attention to his friend. "I'm ready to gamble," he announced.

By midnight the great Shabonee, feared warrior and terror

of the Americans, had won Billy's favorite saddle blanket and two calico shirts. Throughout the next day, Billy had to endure his good-natured gloating. But before the end of the week, Shabonee's mood had changed.

He slumped down next to Billy on the tree-lined ridge overlooking the fort. "Some of the warriors are leaving. Our men want to fight, but they complain that there is nothing to do except watch the Redcoats fire their cannon."

Billy had been watching the Americans through a spyglass. He could see the tops of their heads as they moved along their trenches safe from sniper fire. He swept the spyglass along the perimeter of the fort. The green wood used for the palisade had proved remarkably strong. The British cannon had barely dented the stockade walls.

"That is just what the Americans are hoping for. It is what they have done to us time after time," Billy said. He handed the spyglass to Shabonee so his friend could see for himself. "There must be some way to get the men to stay."

"If we could fight the Americans man to man, they would stay. Tecumseh is talking to General Proctor now about a plan to lure the Americans out."

"He won't listen," Billy predicted.

Frustration had grown between Tecumseh and General Proctor like a festering wound. Whenever Tecumseh suggested a new battle plan or some tactic that might draw the Americans from their fort, Proctor refused even to listen.

Last night, Billy had heard Tecumseh's angry voice coming from Proctor's tent. "Why are your ears deaf to me?" he had said. "We know that more Kentuckians will be here soon. We must act quickly."

Finally, however, to everyone's surprise, the Americans left their fort. Tired of being stung by the British cannon, they sent a contingent of soldiers to capture Proctor's artillery.

It was what Tecumseh had been waiting for. He leaped onto a rock and cried to his men, "Here is our chance! I hear the voices of our brothers who died at Fallen Timbers. They urge us to fight for our land."

The warriors drank his words like thirsty men. Tecumseh directed some of them to guard the river where the reinforcements from Kentucky were expected. Others he took with him to fight the Americans.

Fighting commenced quickly. For three hours it raged, the deafening clap of rifle fire echoing weirdly from the riverside bluffs. The Indians lowered their guns only when their weapons grew too hot to touch, or when clouds of smoke obscured their vision.

Billy had returned to the British encampment to confer with Matthew Elliott. Suddenly one of the young Shawnee braves sprinted into the clearing. "Sauganash, hurry, you are needed!"

"Someone needs a translator," Matthew Elliott guessed.

"No," the youth gasped. "I mean . . . yes . . ."

The boy was flustered. He was only about sixteen, and this was his first battle. Billy remembered how he had felt during his own first skirmishes a year ago.

"The Kentuckians . . ." the boy said.

Billy climbed on Kumari and drew the boy up behind him. "Come on. You can tell me on the way!"

As they raced through the woods, the runner told the story in bits and pieces.

"The soldiers from Kentucky came . . ."

The mare jumped a fallen tree.

"Tecumseh surrounded and captured them. He told the warriors to bring them here, but . . ." The boy was still out of breath from his long race to the encampment.

"Prisoners . . . tortured!"

"Was a runner sent to tell Tecumseh?" Billy shouted.

"Yes."

Billy was trying to make sense of the story as he drove Kumari onward. As they neared the place where the prisoners had been taken, they heard the cries of injured men. They arrived just as Tecumseh burst from the forest from the other direction. Together, they raced their horses to where the American troops were being held.

There, huddled together in a frightened mass, eighty prisoners awaited their fate. They'd been beaten badly, having been made to run a vicious gantlet, and now some of the braves were killing them one by one. General Proctor was at the scene. He stood aside and watched dispassionately as one warrior clubbed a captive. Billy jumped from his horse and entered the fray, dodging tomahawks and knives.

"Cowards, all of you!" he shouted. "*Ke'go*—stop!"

An Ojibwa warrior, garishly painted with red and black circles around his eyes, pushed Billy aside and thrust his knife into a prisoner.

Suddenly Tecumseh flew past Billy. He swung his war club and dealt the disobedient warrior a shattering blow to the head. He fell dead to the ground.

Then the Shawnee war chieftain turned to the others, who stood frozen with surprise. "Now, you want to kill all these prisoners, do you?" He brandished his club menacingly in the air. "First you must kill me, and then you can do as you please. Maybe some of you will die in the effort."

They fell back before his authority.

"Did we not direct in council that prisoners at our mercy were not to be tortured or slain? Did we not acknowledge that such cruelty was the act of frightened men? Where is your bravery now? What has become of my warriors? You are to fight in battle to desperation, but you are never to redden your hands in the blood of prisoners!

"Why," he shouted, turning rigidly to General Proctor, "have you allowed your prisoners to be killed in cold blood?"

Proctor clutched the lapels of his scarlet coat. "Sir, your Indians cannot be commanded," he said, tilting his head back arrogantly.

"Not by cowards," Tecumseh said, enunciating each word. "Take these prisoners to a place where they will be safe."

When Proctor failed to move, Tecumseh shouted, *"Begone!"* He threw up his hands in anger as if to frighten away a flea-bitten mongrel. "You are unfit to command. Go and put on petticoats."

Billy drew a deep breath. His heart seemed to have begun beating again. The remaining captives stared at Tecumseh, astounded by the scene they had just witnessed. Had an Indian savage saved them when a British general would not?

When night fell, it became clear that, although the Americans had lost far more men than either the British or the Indians, Fort Meigs had held, and Harrison remained unharmed behind its sturdy walls.

Billy sat with his back against a tree trunk picking at his

meal of salt pork and biscuits. He mulled over the day's events. The big guns had failed, some of their own men had acted despicably, and Proctor had again proven both his inability to lead and his contempt for the Indians. They had accomplished nothing.

17 · BEFORE ALL THE LEAVES FALL

*T*he flame of hope, which had burned so brightly after their victories in Mackinac, Chicago, and Detroit, began to flicker.

Following a poorly planned attack in which one hundred of his men were mown down by American cannon, Proctor lost heart. He shouted, "Have the buglers sound the retreat! There shall be no more British offensives in the Northwest Territory while I command His Majesty's forces."

Retreating to his gunboats moored in the river below, he fled with his troops to Fort Malden, vowing never again to step on American soil.

"What frightened sparrows they are," Tecumseh remarked, as the ships sailed from their sight.

Abandoned by the Redcoats, Tecumseh and his men returned to the British stronghold overland. They rode back to the north shore of the lake through prairie and marshland under the watchful eyes of soaring eagles. As the days passed, more and more of the warriors drifted away. They grumbled that the British had abandoned them, afraid of the Americans.

Each morning, Billy counted the hoofprints of their horses disappearing into the distance. Each night there were fewer campfires. The magnificent fighting force was melting away like wax before the summer sun.

After they returned to their village near Fort Malden, Tecumseh began fasting in the hope of drawing closer to the spirit world. He needed wisdom, he said, to lead the people. Soon his cheekbones jutted from his face, and his eyes were aflame with intensity.

An insufferable late-summer heat had descended on the land. Even the air seemed to weigh them down. During this time, a disturbing change began to creep over Tecumseh. He grew closer to the spirit world, and as he did so, he seemed to fade from the world of men, as if he were vanishing ghostlike in the August haze.

One evening, he walked with Billy to the hillock overlooking the herd of horses. On the way, a little girl dashed boldly up to Billy, sweetly pestering him until he held her by the wrists and swung her gaily around as she giggled. Billy laughed, too, thinking it had been a long time since he had done so.

He joined Tecumseh at the summit of the hill, where the Shawnee leader sat watching the horses. The animals milled quietly in the distance, their tails swishing at flies.

"You've been solemn for many days," Billy said.

"The obstacles we face are many," Tecumsch said, his gaze fixed on the horses. "The force we assembled in the spring is breaking apart like clods of earth from the storm-battered lake cliffs. Many of the warriors say the Great Spirit has turned his face from us."

"God hasn't turned from us. How could God not want us to

have a home? It is General Proctor. He's a coward," Billy said with disgust. "There's no fire in his belly." He plucked at a blade of grass and chewed it. "Every battle he's led has gone against us."

The only bright spot to greet them when they reached Fort Malden had been the presence of the young one-armed naval hero, Lieutenant Barclay. He could often be seen on the deck of his flagship, the *Detroit*, as she rocked in the harbor. With his empty sleeve pinned to his shoulder, he strode from bow to stern resolutely issuing orders. He was determined to beat the Americans on Lake Erie. He struck up a friendship with Tecumseh and recruited some of his men as naval sharp-shooters.

It was a breezy September morning when Tecumseh and Billy watched the British navy set sail. They knew the Americans under Commodore Oliver Hazard Perry had assembled their ships near the little islands at the western end of the lake.

"When you see me return," Barclay said, after he ordered the anchor raised, "you will know that we have been victorious."

The sails of the *Detroit* billowed proudly as she led the way downriver. Proctor paced back and forth along the wharf, muttering to his officers that this battle would be decisive.

By afternoon, they heard the thunder of the shipboard cannon, and puffs of smoke resembling cloud formations appeared on the horizon. For two hours the booming sounded, the artillery roaring time after time with barely a moment's respite. Then all was silent. Those left behind onshore could only look to one another and wonder about the outcome. A wall of smoke like a fog bank rolled toward them, stinging their throats and making their eyes water.

Barclay did not return that night.

The next day Tecumseh returned to the beach to watch for him. Scanning the empty horizon with his spyglass, he searched for an hour. But no ships dotted the water. He besieged Proctor with questions. "Our fleet has gone out. We know they have fought. We have heard the great guns. But we know nothing of what has happened to our father with one arm."

The general could not or would not answer him.

Tecumseh tried to encourage his own men in the councils that followed, but clouds covered his words. "What we begin now," he said to Billy, Shabonee, and the other chiefs who'd gathered around, "is the beginning of the end. This war will be decided before all the leaves fall. At that time, Grandmother Kokomthena will gather me up in her net, and I will depart from you for another world."

When he saw the consternation upon their faces, he said, "Do not be disheartened. We can still accomplish what we've set out to do."

As long as Tecumseh was alive, there remained a chance they could achieve a homeland. But if Tecumseh died, they all knew there was none who could replace him. More than anything, Billy wanted to protect Tecumseh. If he lived, the Shawnee chief would kill Harrison. Then the Indians would return to Ohio. They would have a home to call their own. It would be a land where they could hunt and fish, a place where they could build their *wegiwehs* and live in safety. He would make it a gift to Jane.

Finally, eight days after Barclay sailed away, Proctor admitted at a meeting held with Tecumseh and dozens of his warriors and war chiefs that the Americans had been victorious. He had known for several days.

"Our ships had difficulty maneuvering," he explained as he paced nervously, "and the Americans took advantage. Lieutenant Barclay was badly wounded in the fight and had to be carried belowdecks." Proctor's hair was uncombed, and his coat was buttoned crooked. "The British fleet," he continued in a shaky voice, "has been captured by Perry. It will be used against us to ferry Harrison's entire army here in a matter of days. Since we are not prepared to face a massive American assault, I have decided to burn Fort Malden and retreat."

Confusion erupted. Shouting filled the hall. The Indians were enraged at Proctor's actions. He had withheld information from them and made decisions without seeking their advice in council. Only Tecumseh's upraised hand kept them from attacking the general. But even Tecumseh could barely control his fury.

Holding the wampum belt he had draped over his shoulder, he spoke sternly to the British general. "Listen! When war was declared, our father stood up and gave us the tomahawk and told us that he was ready to strike the Americans, that he wanted our aid, and that he would certainly get back our lands which the Americans had taken from us.

"You always told us you would never draw your foot off British ground, but now, Father, we see that you are drawing back, and we are sorry to see our father doing so without seeing the enemy. We must compare our father's conduct to a fat dog that carries its tail on its back but, when affrighted, drops it between his legs and runs off."

Proctor stiffened with rage at this insult. The muscle along his pale jawbone quivered.

"Father, listen!" Tecumseh continued. "The Americans have not yet defeated us by land. We therefore wish to remain here and fight our enemy should they make their appearance. If they beat us, we will then retreat with our father."

He strode up and down the center aisle of the meeting hall where they had gathered. Morning light flooded through the open windows, and he moved from sunlight to shadow to sunlight. The angry murmuring among his men had ceased. They gave him their full attention. He drew his listeners to him with his expressive hands, his face, his modulated voice, and the power of the message he shared.

"Father," he said, speaking more quietly now, "you have got the arms and the ammunition that our Great Father sent to his children. If you have an idea of going away, give them to us and you may go and welcome! For us, our lives are in the hands of the Great Spirit. We are determined to defend our lands and, if it be his will, we wish to leave our bones upon them."

Shouts of agreement shook the walls.

"Why do you prepare to run," Tecumseh asked, "before you have even seen the flash of his sword in the sunlight? It is not a good thing to run before the shadow he throws. Give me the militia, and with them and my own people, we will meet Harrison. We will strike him. The Detroit River will redden with their blood. We will fight them foot by foot and tree by tree. For the Indians, whose land this is, I say this: We will not give up the fight against Harrison, and sooner or later all that will be left of us is our bones. It is better that we leave our bones in the lands of our fathers than in lands that know us not and where we are strangers."

But this was not General Proctor's home, and he was not willing to leave his bones here to please this savage who obviously knew nothing about keeping a large army supplied. He argued military strategy. "My scouts reliably inform me that the Americans plan to land at several points. We will be surrounded by a superior force of eight thousand men, and we will be given no mercy."

Tecumseh only shook his head and said contemptuously, "I am in the company of cowards who fear the very wind that brings scent of an enemy."

Proctor continued to press his case. "Food is scarce. The Americans have captured most of our artillery pieces from Barclay's ships. Would it not be wiser to retreat along the Thames River to where it becomes too shallow for Perry's fleet to follow, and there make a stand against the Americans in a place that is strange to them?"

They argued for hours. But Tecumseh could not sway Proctor, and in the end, he was forced to agree to this plan.

That night, as he met in council with the other chiefs, he said, "My brothers, I will not leave you. My home is on the battlefield, and I have no fear of death."

His closest allies promised to remain by his side.

Shabonee said, "Tecumseh, you are my leader and my friend. As long as one or the other of us should remain alive, I will never leave you."

Billy, too, vowed to remain. "Should the very hills bury me, I will keep my word to you."

The others, each in his own language, expressed similar thoughts.

The next day a warm sun shone from a crisp blue sky. Billy found Tecumseh as the Shawnee emerged from his *wegiweh*. They fetched their horses and watered them in the stream.

They had no desire to stay near Fort Malden and watch Proctor set it ablaze. Instead, Billy rode with Tecumseh to the lake one more time. Earlier they had ridden to watch for Barclay's return. Now they scouted the horizon for signs of Harrison and the fleet.

The leaves of the cottonwood trees sailed gently through the air on a pleasant breeze, and now and then a chevron of geese honked as they winged their way south. The peacefulness of the earth and all her creatures belied the violence that had occurred not long before. From the shoreline, Tecumseh and Billy could see the bodies of sailors killed in last week's naval battle floating in the water. They recognized the drowned by their colors: the British regulars dressed in their scarlet coats, Barclay's marines in gray, and the Americans in their blue jackets.

Tecumseh galloped his horse along the shore, sometimes dashing back and forth the entire front of the beach, sometimes stopping and staring across the water as if to reconnoiter.

Billy dismounted and allowed Kumari to wander through the scrub grass. Standing among the cottonwood and pine trees, he scanned the horizon. He could see nothing. Laying aside his good scarlet coat with its British Indian Department insignia, he climbed branch by branch nearly to the top of a pine tree. From there, the scent of sap mingled with the fresh breeze blowing off the lake. Before him, the water stretched endlessly. Using the spyglass, he slowly studied the scene from east to west. A tiny speck of white came into view, and then another and another, until a dozen ships sailed into sight. He recognized Barclay's flagship, the *Detroit*, and called down to Tecumseh.

"Yes, I see her, too, Sauganash," Tecumseh said. "Look at the flag that flies from her mast."

Billy lifted the glass again. It was not the British Union Jack but the American Stars and Stripes that snapped in the wind. Now more ships appeared, sixteen major vessels plus many smaller open boats. As they hove into view, Billy could see each deck swarming with American soldiers. The reports were true. Harrison was invading Canada with a colossal force.

"This is why Proctor is fleeing Fort Malden in such haste," Billy said, making his way back down the tree.

Tecumseh replied calmly, "Our lives are in the hands of the Great Spirit. Harrison is coming, and I must face him. One of us will die soon." He took a deep breath and exhaled slowly as if cleansing himself. "I feel the Great Spirit calling me, Sauganash. I think it is I who will die."

Billy felt the warm caress of the sun on his face, and the sweet-smelling breeze from the lake whipped his hair. The sky was blue and the water dark blue, with whitecaps skittering like diamonds over it. Why did its surface have to be marred by death, and by the presence of such an enemy?

18 · WESHECAT-TOO-WEH

With heavy hearts, they turned their horses away from the shore and followed the retreating army of the British and Indians. General Proctor had indeed burned Fort Malden to the ground to prevent the Americans from using it as a stronghold. The black smoke from its flaming timbers stung their nostrils. Riding behind Tecumseh, Billy passed the ruins soberly. This had been his home. He knew the headquarters, the barracks, and the storerooms. His own father had helped design it. Its destruction reminded him of Tippecanoe.

The sky, which had been so clear that morning, darkened with clouds. Over the next several days, a steady rain fell, making the trail nearly impassable. The progress of the fleeing army was agonizingly slow. The Redcoats pushed and pulled their supply wagons and gun carriages through ankle-deep mud. The Indians had the added burden of leading their wives and children and their old people, many of whom struggled on foot.

Scouts raced back and forth on wild-eyed horses, reporting

that Harrison had occupied Detroit and soon after that Amherstburg and the remains of Fort Malden.

He won't be satisfied with our retreat, Billy thought. *He wants to crush the British and the Indians once and for all.*

With a group of hand-picked braves, including Billy, Tecumseh fought an almost continual rearguard action to delay the Americans. If Proctor wouldn't fight, their first goal must be to give their people time to reach a place of safety. But without the British to lend their support, Tecumseh's war party was little more than flies biting the rump of a charging buffalo. Now and then, they would spot General Harrison on his white stallion as he urged his cavalry through the woods. They could hear his strong voice shouting orders. But whenever they aimed their rifles, he seemed to disappear from their sight.

When Proctor learned of Harrison's speed, his flight became even more disorganized. He abandoned the valuable baggage wagons and supplies of ammunition, and hastened away from the pursuing Americans. The British even left behind two gunboats filled with ammunition on the Thames River.

Tecumseh urged Proctor to stop and make a stand.

"Harrison has over five thousand men pursuing us," Proctor snapped, clearly fearful of confronting such a force. "Chief, the Kentucky horsemen ride like blasted demons, and their sharpshooters can hit a mark at three hundred yards."

"They are only men, and our bullets can stop them," Tecumseh said.

Day after day, Tecumseh beseeched Proctor to act like a man. Finally, the general agreed to stop and fight. But that night, unbeknownst to the Indians, Proctor allowed his fears to overwhelm him. Once more he fled, retreating upriver with his

Redcoats. In the morning, when they learned what had happened, Tecumseh's people had no choice but to follow.

Late one afternoon, after they had been on the trail for more than a week, Tecumseh sent most of his warriors ahead to make camp. Promising to join them at nightfall, he remained behind with two hundred of his men. These few would face the vanguard of Harrison's army, one thousand mounted Kentuckians. Always the strategist, Tecumseh hid his men at the fording place of a creek. Patiently, they waited for the Americans to cross.

As the sun began to lower, the Kentuckians rode into view, and their horses splashed into the stream.

"AI-AI-AI-AI!" Tecumseh's chilling war cry ripped through the woods. The Indians opened fire. The horses plunged and reared, creating fountains of spray in the water. The Americans frantically wheeled their animals about and retreated to cover. For two hours the firing continued until a thick pall of smoke wafted among the trees.

At nightfall, with only the moon to light their way, the Indians retreated to their camp. As was his custom, Tecumseh was the last to leave the battlefield, guarding their rear flank.

They had succeeded in slowing the Long Knives, but every man knew their position was growing desperate. With each passing day, the Americans had narrowed the gap between the hunter and the hunted.

After they'd rejoined the rest, Billy saw the blood on Tecumseh's sleeve. "You've been hurt," he said with alarm.

"It is not serious," the chief protested, fingering the tear in his shirt.

But Billy saw by his clenched jaw that Tecumseh was in pain.

He washed the wound and tended it, using the buzzard down he kept in his medicine pouch to stanch the flow of blood. Tearing his own calico shirt to use as a bandage, Billy wrapped it.

When Billy finished, Tecumseh nodded appreciatively. "*Ni-aweh.*" Then he motioned for his closest friends and allies to sit with him around the campfire. His mood was solemn.

"You are my friends, my people. I love you too well to see you sacrificed in an unequal contest from which no good can result. I would dissuade you from fighting this fight, encourage you to leave now, this night, for there is no victory ahead now, only sorrow." His compassionate gaze fell upon each one of the men in this small core of warriors who had risked death with him so often. "Yet, time after time, even until tonight, you have made known to me that it is your desire to fight the Americans here, and so I am willing to go with my people and be guided by their wishes."

"What else can we do? We must continue to fight," Billy said. "It's the only way."

"Sauganash, a war leader does not sacrifice his men when there is no chance of success. Harrison is upon us. He has more men than we can count. The Long Knives will reach us when the sun rises. If I can find Harrison and kill him, perhaps his men will scatter. But if I fall in battle tomorrow before we are assured of the victory, flee the battlefield immediately. You must then lead the people to safety."

One of the war chiefs complained once more of Proctor.

"Yes," Tecumseh agreed, "he is very different from our friend Brock. When General Brock was in command, he used to say, 'Tecumseh, *come* and fight the Americans,' but General Proctor always says, 'Tecumseh, *go* and fight the Americans.'" The Shawnee warrior glanced over at Billy, knowing that perhaps he alone of his men would understand the real meaning behind the subtle and cruel choice of words.

Tecumseh gave away his most cherished possessions that night. A British sword he presented to Shabonee. To another chief he gave a fine tomahawk. To others Tecumseh promised a rifle and a knife.

He had sent Cat Pouncing ahead with Tenskwatawa to relative safety with the main body of Indians. Now he asked that his sword be given to his son in time, when the youth became a noted warrior. Shabonee promised that it would be done. Tecumseh turned to Billy. "This is for you, Sauganash." He placed in Billy's hand one of the pistols that had been given to him by Isaac Brock, which Billy had admired so enthusiastically a year ago. Billy ran his fingers along the engraved brass, which shone warmly in the firelight. During the past year, Tecumseh had rarely gone into battle without it. That it should be entrusted to him made Billy ache with pride and sorrow. He felt a stab of pain in his throat again, not unlike the old knife wound.

"*Niaweh*," he said quietly.

For himself, Tecumseh kept only his silver-mounted rifle and a war club.

Billy dwelt on the predictions Tecumseh had made about his own death. At this very moment, they sat among the fallen leaves of autumn. He tried to read Tecumseh's face. There was no sign of fear on the Shawnee warrior's features. To the contrary, the pained expression was gone, and Tecumseh spoke with great serenity.

"It is my last wish to face Harrison tomorrow and be the death of him before he is the death of me."

The next day, October 5, 1813, Tecumseh's force of five hundred braves met up with Proctor. The general's face was pale. Once more he suggested they retreat. But when Tecumseh glared at him, he halted short.

"No, you will stop here," Tecumseh demanded. "You will act like a man. If you run one more time, I promise you I will take my men and leave. You will then face Harrison alone. If we are beaten, we will leave our bones here together."

His disgust was plain in his voice.

Proctor, shamed before his officers, reluctantly agreed. With Tecumseh, he walked the site to see how best to deploy their men. They chose an area near the river where a forest of oak trees towered above them. The water protected their flank, and swampy thickets nearby would slow the advance of American horsemen should the enemy choose to ride from that direction. The forest would provide cover. They could defend themselves, at least for a time. The British dragged their single cannon to the middle of the lane that wound through the area.

"Encourage your soldiers at the big gun to have stout hearts, since the enemy will push strongest at that gun to silence it," Tecumseh said.

He walked down the line of red-coated men, shaking hands with each of the officers. Speaking boldly to help them bear up, Tecumseh said, "*Weshecat-too-weh*—be brave." To others, he said, "Be strong," or, "Shoot straight." He stopped when he reached Colonel Calder. After embracing him warmly, he said quietly, "Our sons will be tested this day."

"They shall not be found wanting," Billy's father said with confidence. Earlier, he had requested and received permission from General Proctor to take his men, Calder's Rangers, and fight by the side of the Indians.

Continuing on, Tecumseh reached Proctor. When he noted the British officer's apprehension, Tecumseh's attitude softened. "Father, tell your men to be firm and all will be well," he said reassuringly.

He then led his warriors into the woods and positioned them where some thickets and a few overturned trees provided concealment.

Billy strode by Tecumseh's side under a lacy canopy of gold autumn leaves. He worried about this British force. They'd been on half rations for several days and were growing disheartened. Everyone knew, too, that they were badly outnumbered by the Americans. Worst of all, His Majesty's army had no leader to inspire them.

"They are just like sheep with their wool tangled and fastened in the bushes," Tecumseh said when they were out of earshot of the Redcoats. "And as fearful," he added, shaking his head. "They cannot fight. The Americans will brush them all away like chaff before the wind."

Billy nodded. He knew the British, led by a man they couldn't trust, would find it difficult when they most needed to be brave. Only his father's Rangers could be counted upon to hold firm.

"Tecumseh, whatever the British do, I will stand by you to the last. I'll remain at my position until you order me to abandon it."

Before he finished speaking, Billy sensed a terrible disturbance, as though good and evil spirits were battling in the air over their heads. Tecumseh seemed to feel it, too. Stopping once or twice, he had sniffed the air like an animal suspecting the presence of enemies. With his face painted red and black, the colors of war and death, he appeared as an otherworldly spirit himself. Years ago, he had told Billy of the evil Matchemoneto, the demon most determined to do him harm. In response, he had fasted often and prayed to the Great Spirit to lead him on the right path. It was the Great Spirit who had taught Tecumseh to refrain from torture and to keep the welfare of his people uppermost in his thoughts.

Now, as they returned to their comrades, Billy felt these enormous forces of good and evil in combat around them as if there was a struggle not only for a homeland but for their very souls. It was at that moment that they heard the whine of a rifle ball. Instantly, each warrior tensed.

Tecumseh staggered back as though hit by a bullet. He grabbed the left side of his chest. His face was contorted with pain. But strangely, there was no blood on his hand when he examined it and no tear in his shirt. He had been hit, and yet he was unharmed. His companions, each of whom had clearly heard the sound of rifle fire, stared at him, frightened. Tecumseh was shaken by the occurrence but quickly regained his composure. Still, it was a bad omen. He knew the end was near. "It is a sign from Matchemoneto," was all he said, resigned to what lay ahead.

"Leave, Tecumseh. Live to fight another day," Billy urged.

"No," Tecumseh said. "I will hear no more such talk."

"Then stand behind me and let me be your bodyguard."

Tecumseh placed his hand on Billy's shoulder. A slight smile played on his lips. "No, Sauganash, you and I will fight side by side."

"All . . . is not lost," Billy said hesitantly.

"No, all is not lost."

"We can beat these Long Knives. We can retake Ohio, and it will be a home for us forever."

"If it is the will of the Great Spirit," Tecumseh said calmly.

Then they waited, every nerve and muscle alert, knowing Harrison was coming. They strained their ears for a sign of the enemy. Billy's heart pounded against his ribs. The fast, which he had begun the previous night, heightened all his senses. His sight was like the hawk's, his hearing like the wolf's. As they kept silent, listening only to the sound of their own breathing, the distant sound of bugles pierced the air like a faraway cry. Each man looked to the others. The battle would commence shortly. They readied their weapons.

Suddenly Billy realized Tecumseh was watching him. When Billy looked at him questioningly, Tecumseh waited some time before whispering, "Sauganash, I want you to go to General Proctor." Again he hesitated as if unsure of what to say. "Wait with him . . . and bring any messages he has for me."

Billy knew that Tecumseh said this only to spare him. The warrior wanted to save Billy's life when the fighting became fierce.

"No."

"Sauganash," Tecumseh said, chuckling for the first time that day, because he knew that Billy understood his reasons, "it is true what they say of you—that you are bullheaded." Then he became more serious. "You accepted me as a war chief and have never yet disobeyed me in anything I asked you to do.

Now I am ordering you to do this thing. I have always been able to trust in the loyalty of my men."

Billy drew a deep breath. "I won't disappont you, Tecumseh."

He would obey. It was his duty. Racing to the rear lines where Proctor had stationed himself, he found there were no messages from the British command post. Indeed, it seemed the general was quietly preparing to retreat again. Billy returned to Tecumseh's side within minutes.

He told the chief what he had seen. Then he said, "Please don't send me away again." His eyes were burning with intense emotion.

A second blare of bugles drew their attention to a small force of mounted Americans racing through the trees. Tecumseh raised the war cry and leveled his weapon. The Indians and Colonel Calder's Rangers fired in unison. The Americans fell back, but the reprieve was short-lived, as a larger force of more than one hundred Kentucky horsemen followed. Furious fighting broke out. Tecumseh repeatedly sighted down the barrel of his rifle, squeezed the trigger, and then with lightning-quick precision, reloaded. The crack of gunfire sounded all around them. The warrior next to Billy was struck in the head by a bullet and died. A few minutes later, a Wyandot chieftain was killed in close fighting when the vanguard of the Americans entered the fray. Tecumseh signaled for his men to fall back and regroup.

He'd torn off his deerskin hunting shirt in the heat of battle. Now he leaped bare-chested over fallen tree trunks, jumping from cover to cover. The scarlet band he wore around his brow could be seen like a cardinal flitting from tree to tree as he raced among them. Over the report of gunfire, they heard his powerful voice calling to them. "Be brave! Be strong! Be brave!" His words checked their fear and stiffened their resolve.

The American troops poured toward them, raising their own cry, "Remember the River Raisin!"

Billy instinctively reached up and touched the scar on the side of his neck.

Tecumseh shouted at him, "Come!"

Billy fell back and found another position to defend.

As the autumn sun began to lower in the sky, a Shawnee runner arrived with the news that General Proctor had retreated again, leaving behind a force of several hundred British soldiers. These had been surrounded by the Americans and forced to surrender. He warned that Harrison's men were now using the same tactic against Tecumseh in the woods.

"We can still beat them!" Billy cried obstinately. "We don't need Proctor."

"It is time to fall back, Sauganash," Tecumseh said, pointing through the trees at several enemy soldiers, some on horseback, others on foot, trying to outflank them.

Billy reluctantly left his place. In the distance, through the golden forest, he made out the blurred forms of American soldiers running to cut them off. Beyond them, Kentucky horsemen were regrouping in a clearing, readying for a charge. A familiar white stallion carried General Harrison, and Billy could hear the voice of the man who had sworn to take the Northwest Territory from the Indians as he bellowed orders to his cavalry.

When Tecumseh saw that white horse and the general who rode it, he stopped by an uprooted tree and primed his rifle.

He would not let this opportunity pass. *"Go!"* he shouted at Billy.

The pop and crack of rifle fire grew more frequent. The noise came from three sides now. They were nearly surrounded. They must fall back quickly to escape. As he retreated toward the British lines, Billy heard an explosion. A telltale puff of smoke rose from a sniper's lair a hundred yards away. Billy spun around and was appalled to see Tecumseh staggering toward him.

"Are you hurt?" he cried.

"I am shot!" Tecumseh called out to him.

The Shawnee leaned on his rifle, using it as a staff. His other hand clutched at his heart, the same spot where the phantom bullet had struck him earlier. He took a few steps, then sat down heavily on the fallen log, his breathing labored. Tecumseh weakly lifted his hand in a final parting before he slumped to the ground.

*B*illy flew to his side.

Blood decorated the Shawnee's chest like war paint. Billy cradled his friend and leader in his arms. He could do nothing more. There was not enough buzzard down in the wide world to stanch the bleeding. Tecumseh's breathing slowed and then ceased. Billy gently laid him on the ground. He quickly covered him with leaves to hide him from the Americans, for the Kentuckians had threatened to mutilate the Shawnee should his body ever fall into their hands. Lifting his face to the sky, Billy howled in anguish. He sang the Shawnee death song to warn the others.

Instantly, concealed warriors, clad in deerskin, who only a moment earlier had been invisible, emerged and retreated. They withdrew up a slope, their moccasins stirring the leaves that covered the earth. Sprinting past umber-colored oak and blood-red sumac, they hastened from the area of combat. As they fell back, Billy caught sight of young Cat Pouncing. The boy had only recently become a warrior in the Shawnee tradition, and he'd been instructed to remain on the fringe of the fighting. He had been some distance away and was unaware of his father's death. Billy took the youth by the arm and fled with him through the forest.

When they reached a place of temporary safety, Billy quietly took him aside and had him sit down. He squatted by the boy's side and placed his hand on the lad's shoulder. "Your father was a brave man," Billy said. The wild look on Cat Pouncing's face told Billy that he was beginning to guess what had happened. The boy's hands started to shake badly, and Billy held them firmly between his own to quell their trembling.

"He is with us no longer. His last journey has begun. You know that he will be restored to life in the other world."

"What will we do?" Cat Pouncing asked.

"We will go on, as your father would have wished."

That evening, Billy helped establish a camp at a safe distance from the Americans where the exhausted survivors could rest. There, it was confirmed that Proctor had fled, leaving behind over six hundred of his own men to be captured. His Indian allies and their families had been abandoned. They had been betrayed once again.

When it grew quite dark, Billy took a handful of trusted warriors and crept silently through the woods within sight of the American campfires. He led them to the spot where Tecumseh had fallen. They retrieved the body of their chief and buried it near a stream in the Shawnee fashion, with his head to the west and his face painted so that the Great Spirit would know him. A medicine man chanted the prayers for the dead and reminded them that in four days Tecumseh's spirit would reach its destination.

Later, though he was more tired than he had ever felt before, Billy found that he could not sleep. Sitting with his back against a tree trunk, he closed his eyes and tried to shut out the sound of weeping that hung over the wretched camp. They had lost a courageous and selfless leader, a man who could never be replaced. Others, too, had died that day, and many women and children mourned husbands and fathers. Billy glanced over at the tearstained face of Cat Pouncing, who'd finally fallen asleep. The feeling of hopelessness was beyond anything he had yet endured.

Billy felt as if his own heart had been torn from his chest and devoured by the enemy. What he had dreaded most, what he had loathed to even contemplate—the death of Tecumseh—had come to pass. They had lost the military struggle. Only Tecumseh could hold them together. The British would not back them again after this failure. It would be hopeless to continue the fight. And it would be wrong to needlessly sacrifice their young men in a war they could no longer win. They had truly lost Ohio and everything Billy had dreamed of for so long. Now what would they do?

He lifted his face to the stars above. The first of the winter constellations appeared at the horizon. Soon the world would sleep again under a blanket of snow. Billy envied the animals that would burrow into soft underground dens and drowse while the wind raged above them. He longed to sleep and to forget the things he had seen.

He thought, too, of everyone who had tried to open his mind over the years. He had been too stubborn, too unwilling to consider other paths. He recalled the book Père Jean-Paul had given him by St. Ignatius. That man had been powerful long after his death. Even without a rifle, he had been strong.

His army of black robes had done much good. Billy thought of Jane. She was right. It was the family that created a home. That was more important than a place. He thought of his father and mother. Colonel Calder had survived and eluded capture. He had skillfully managed to keep his Rangers intact. Billy realized with a growing awareness and gratitude how his father had nurtured him. His mother, too, had taught him so much. She, more than most, had a right to be bitter. Instead, she had quietly created a new home in a strange place. He had not fully understood it before. Now he knew: home meant family. That was why Tecumseh had urged that not a single warrior be wasted in a battle doomed to fail. For each warrior was a husband perhaps, or a father, or a brother. That was what made the Indian nations strong: their sense of family. He had indeed been bullheaded, thinking that the only way he could defend his people was as a warrior.

Tecumseh had followed one path, and it had been a noble path while there was hope. But now Billy must follow another trail. With Tecumseh dead, the military struggle was futile. He must find another way to serve.

Why did I think there was only one way? he wondered. Now he would find Jane and beg her to marry him. He wanted to have sons and daughters with Jane. He would teach his children the skills Tecumseh, and Père Jean-Paul, and his father and mother had taught him. By doing so, he could create his own homeland. Had it not always been this way with the Shawnee and the Miami and the Potawatomi, and the other tribes of the lake country? The land was sacred, it was true, but the family even more so.

The hours passed and Billy watched the constellations

slowly circle the North Star. He decided that night that he would lay down his weapons forever. He would turn from the red path of war and follow the white road of peace. He would fight armed with words alone.

The next morning before dawn broke, Billy roused the demoralized men, women, and children. With the help of his father and Shabonee, and his colleagues in the British Indian Department, he led the bedraggled column of cold, hungry people on their long walk upriver to a place of safety.

The sky was again overcast with leaden clouds, and rain fell throughout the day. Warriors, grief-stricken by the death of Tecumseh, sang the Wolf Chant, a lament traditionally sung as the dead were carried from the battlefield. Children cried fretfully from fatigue. As they followed the road eastward, Billy came across a ragged little girl struggling through the mud. He barely remembered her as the same mischievous child who had once pestered him to play. He dismounted and scooped her up in his arms. Lifting her to his saddle, he led Kumari by the bridle. Another child he carried on his back.

That night, seeing that they were still hungry after having eaten their meager rations, Billy gathered the children around him. He told them a story to take their thoughts from their troubles. It was a story he had once heard Jane tell.

"Many, many years ago," Billy began, "water covered the whole earth. Fish and other sea animals swam in the water, and birds flew over its surface. Then one day an amazing thing happened. A divine woman fell from the sky."

The children's eyes grew wide. Some shook their heads and shouted "No!" in disbelief.

"Yes," Billy assured them. "This is how it was. She called for help and a pair of loons flew up and caught her. They set her on the back of a large turtle."

Billy stopped and poked at the fire until it blazed up again, while the children tugged at his sleeve, asking, "Then what happened?"

"Then the turtle commanded the water creatures to dive down and bring back mud from the bottom," Billy said, continuing the story. "First the beaver dived. But the water was very deep, and he could not reach the bottom. Next the muskrat dived into the water, but he, too, was unable to reach the bottom. Then a snake tried, but he also failed. Finally a little green toad offered to go, but they all laughed at him, saying he was much too weak. But the little green toad persisted. He dived down into the water, kicking his legs behind him."

Billy puffed out his cheeks and drew his arms up and down in imitation of the toad until the boys and girls forgot their hunger pangs and were grinning.

"Deeper and deeper he swam," Billy said. "It was very dark. He could no longer see the light of the sun above him. He was afraid. But do you think he gave up?"

"No!" "Of course not!" the children called out.

Billy looked at their faces. There was the boy he had carried and the girl who'd ridden his mare. He knew many of the others by name, the children of friends. His goal was to get them all to a safe place.

"Go on," they urged, when he had been quiet too long.

"No, he did not give up," Billy said with a smile. "That little toad kept on going until he touched the bottom. He scooped up some mud, then up and up he swam. He thought his chest would burst. At last he reached the surface. The wonderful woman from the sky took the mud and smeared it on the back of the turtle, where it grew, and it grew, and it grew."

Billy spread his hands wider and wider to show how the world took shape.

"And to this day, it is the turtle who holds the world on his back. But it is all due to the courage of the little toad."

He took off his scarlet coat and wrapped it around a boy who sat shivering at his feet.

The next day, they trudged twenty miles through the mud. Billy often made his way back and forth along the column to encourage those who had fallen behind. He carried small children. At noon when they stopped to rest, he built a travois to carry an ailing grandmother. That night, some of the children searched throughout the camp until they found Billy. They begged him to tell them another story. Though he was weary and hungry himself, he cheerfully told them another tale about the beginning of the world.

"Long ago, back when dogs could talk, the Shawnee lived in a foreign land. The Great Spirit declared that he would lead them to a new country filled with streams, and forests, and animals. So, knowing that it was the Great Spirit who led them, they walked right to the edge of the sea."

A little boy climbed onto Billy's lap while his sister stood behind him, wrapping her arms affectionately around Billy's neck. The other children inched closer to him to hear each word.

"The water parted and they walked on the bottom of the sea for many days until they reached this land."

There were shouts of surprise and questions about how such a thing could happen. As Billy answered all their questions, the child on his lap fell asleep. He carried him back to his mother, who opened her blanket and tucked him inside next to her for the night.

At sunset on the third day, the children insisted that Billy come and tell another tale. He decided to tell a story Père Jean-Paul had taught him when Billy was a child himself. Using names the children would know, Billy began, "The Great Spirit created the heavens and the earth. The earth was covered in raging waters and steeped in darkness. So the Great Spirit said, 'Let there be light.' Then He divided the sea from the dry land. Day by day, the Great Spirit created the earth. He created plants and every kind of animal. Then He formed man from the dust on the ground and breathed into his nostrils the breath of life . . ."

Before he could finish, half of the children had fallen asleep from exhaustion. How he pitied them. He knew they dreamed of food and dry clothes; they talked of little else during the day. He had to get them to a place of safety soon.

The next evening, a cold wind blew through the birch forest where they had stopped. Their campfires gave little heat, and they all longed to be in a warm lodge.

Billy had many listeners tonight. Shabonee came, along with Colonel Calder and Matthew Elliott. Children thronged about him while their mothers and fathers stood at the fringe of the circle he'd attracted. A story was expected. Casting about in his mind, Billy remembered a tale Tecumseh had once told.

Tecumseh. The image of the Shawnee chief was ever before him. The knowledge that he was really and truly gone was a constant source of pain to Billy, a permanent ache in his heart. Billy suddenly realized that this was the fourth night since

Tecumseh had died. He had reached his destination in the other world. Was it heaven, Billy wondered. Was it the same place some of the Indians called the happy hunting ground, the land far to the west? Did Tecumseh walk with Isaac Brock? Did he sit by Grandmother Kokomthena's fire eating savory stew from the pot she stirred?

Billy settled himself, and his listeners found places around him. It was difficult for him to begin. A hard lump clogged his throat. But this was a good story, which perhaps they all needed to hear. Billy began slowly:

"The Great Spirit created the first Indians. He formed their bones and muscles. He gave them legs and feet, arms and hands. He gave them eyes with which to see and ears with which to hear. Lastly, he gave them a piece of his heart, which was good, and he mixed it with the hearts they already had, so that a part of their hearts at least would always be good."

A log collapsed on the feeble little fire. Flames blazed up, lighting their faces with a warm glow. Billy saw men and women and children sitting shoulder to shoulder, smiling to remember they had something divine within them. That knowledge would carry them the rest of the way.

He knew he had found the right path.

Epilogue

*C*rossing the Panther's Path is based on the true story of
Billy Caldwell and Tecumseh. All the major events in
the book really happened. The real Billy Caldwell was
both Indian and Irish. Educated by French Jesuits and em-
ployed by John Kinzie, he spoke several languages and assisted
Tecumseh as a translator and warrior. The historical account
of his rescue of the Kinzie family is fascinating, and he was
wounded exactly as described in the Battle of the River Raisin
in 1813. After Tecumseh's death at the Battle of the Thames,
Billy, as a captain in the British Indian Department, led the defeated warriors and their families to safety.

The War of 1812, which was fought not only in the Northwest Territory but also as far south as New Orleans, and as far
east as Washington, D.C., as well as on the high seas, came to
an official close with the signing of the Treaty of Ghent on December 24, 1814. During negotiations, the British argued for
an Indian state to be created, but the Americans refused to
consider it. Not long after that, the last of the Ohio lands was
ceded to the United States.

Believing that the tribes could no longer win, Billy turned from the life of a soldier. Instead, he acted as an Indian agent, a liaison between the American government and the tribal leaders. Returning to Chicago with Shabonee and his people, he built a thriving business as a trader. He settled down with his wife, John Kinzie's half-Indian, half-white niece, and his many children.

His friend Shabonee reached the same conclusion about the futility of warfare. When his people pressed him to continue the fight, claiming the united tribes were as numerous as the trees of the forests, Shabonee answered them by saying, "Yes, and the army of the pale faces you will have to encounter will be as numerous as the leaves on those trees." Together, he and Billy worked hard to solve problems in a peaceful manner.

Billy Caldwell used his skills to help the Potawatomi keep their land in Illinois and Indiana. In turn, that tribe trusted Billy and made him one of its chiefs. For years, he stalled government attempts to claim the area. However, land-hungry settlers continued to press hard for the purchase of farms, and finally the Potawatomi surrendered most of their prairie territory and moved farther west. Billy, who could have remained in his comfortable house on the Chicago River, left everything behind. To reach their new land, he led over seven hundred people on a hard winter journey of two months. Like his mother and father before him, Billy knew a life of exile. His last home was at Trader's Point, near present-day Council Bluffs, Iowa. He died there in 1841 in a cholera epidemic.

A remarkable man, Billy Caldwell was a blend of many cultures. Born on St. Patrick's Day, he was called a good Irish Catholic. His father, from northern Ireland and a friend of the

British, left a lasting impression on his son. Billy once referred to himself as "a true Briton." His Indian friends always called him Sauganash, "Englishman," and he often signed official documents with both his English and his Indian name. He was a lifelong friend of the Jesuits, many of whom were French, and he helped them whenever he could as they established schools and missions across the frontier. Although probably Mohawk on his mother's side, Billy was considered a member of the Potawatomi nation. When he died, tribal leaders petitioned the government to change their name to the Prairie Indians of Caldwell's Band of the Potawatomi.

Billy Caldwell abandoned Tecumseh's dream of reclaiming the Indian homelands through military force, but he continued to admire his friend and leader who had laid down his life for his people. He wrote of him with warmth and respect. The years he'd spent with the Shawnee warrior who was known as the Panther Passing Across instilled in him a spirit of courage and a determination to serve others. Throughout his life, he followed Tecumseh's last advice to him: "Be brave! Be strong!"